Vladimir Torchilin is a University Distinguished Professor of Pharmaceutical Sciences and Director of the Center for Pharmaceutical Biotechnology and Nanomedicine at Northeastern University, Boston. He was born in Moscow (that time Soviet Union), got his scientific degrees from the Moscow State University, and immigrated to the US in 1990. He has published over 650 scientific papers and reviews, written and edited 15 books, holds over 40 patents, and received multiple national and international awards. He is also a writer (member of the Union of Moscow Writers), has multiple publications in leading Russian language literary magazines, and published eight books of short stories in Russian, both in Russia and US. He lives in Boston.

Vladimir Torchilin

THE NETSUKE FROM SAN FRANCISCO

AUSTIN MACAULEY PUBLISHERS™
LONDON • CAMBRIDGE • NEW YORK • SHARJAH

This is a work of fiction. Names, characters, businesses, places, events, locales, and incidents are either the products of the author's imagination or used in a fictitious manner. Any resemblance to actual persons, living or dead, or actual events is purely coincidental.

Ordering Information
Quantity sales: Special discounts are available on quantity purchases by corporations, associations, and others. For details, contact the publisher at the address below.

Publisher's Cataloging-in-Publication data
Torchilin, Vladimir
The Netsuke from San Francisco

ISBN 9798889103561 (Paperback)
ISBN 9798889103578 (Hardback)
ISBN 9798889103585 (ePub e-book)

Library of Congress Control Number: 2023913742

www.austinmacauley.com/us

First Published 2024
Austin Macauley Publishers LLC
40 Wall Street, 33rd Floor, Suite 3302
New York, NY 10005
USA

mail-usa@austinmacauley.com
+1 (646) 5125767

Table of Contents

The Stairs

Life is mostly a dour affair, and you die
in the end.
—*Janusz Leon Wiśniewski*

Twenty-six, twenty-seven, twenty-eight…

And then slower.

Twenty-nine, thirty…

"Jesus, why the whole damn world is made of stairs?! Wherever you go, stairs. Going down to the subway, stairs. Leaving the subway, more stairs. Want to cross the street? You guessed it, stairs again! Museums mean stairs both on the way in and the way out. Well, to be fair, there ARE some elevators out there, but the world is more or less ruled by stairs. Stairs…stairs…stairs."

He tried recalling when this thought had first crossed his mind. Must have been back in London. Yes, probably London, where he loathed the old Tube that, naturally, had been built with no escalators, only endless subterranean passages chock full of stairs, up and down without so much as a second to catch your breath. Granted, London's underground air doesn't generally make for good breathing material; taking it in does little to recover your breath, and the crowd will push you forward with no regard for your desire to take a break. Younger commuters would just keep on treading, setting too high a pace for you to comfortably keep up with, as they don't really mind stairs. That felt especially aggravating at Russell Square station, where you had to brave a devilish number of stairs, well-polished by the collective effort of thousands, or rather millions of feet, just to get to the elevator, which would finally deliver you from the Underground. Every single time he had to visit London for business, his company would—without fail—book him into the same hotel at that godforsaken Russell Square, which, in time, only enhanced his nightmares with vivid images of the stairs down there. Come to think of it; it's really weird how the plainest specimen of a staircase can become perfect nightmare fuel. It doesn't even require any especially cruel details—just for the said staircase to grow taller and taller until its end, and the path leading to the elevator becomes so far away that you can barely make it out anymore. In those moments, he felt himself a miserable, bloated Sisyphean creature, forever destined to drag its bulk over soiled masonry stairs, and at that moment, he would wake up short of breath amid a bunch of blankets positively dripping with sweat.

Or did it happen in Paris? The lady who had kept him company that day (or was it the other way around?) would have him hastily cross the Champs-Élysées through pedestrian tunnels that were sure to welcome him with at least twenty stairs on the way down and just as many on the way up, which had repeated innumerable times, as she wouldn't hear of skipping a single one of the lavish boutiques peppering both sides of the avenue. When at one point, he had found himself trailing her by at least half a tunnel, she had stopped and waited for him to catch up, tapping her foot on the cracked floor tiles like a horse antsy to be ridden. Once he reached her, she had been appalled at the delay for fear of missing something and reacted to his lamentations about the torturous stairs by hissing a quiet but distinct "drop dead already, will you?" They had been nearing a breakup back then anyway, but those stairs made another deep imprint on his memory.

In a word, quite a while had passed since he had started noticing it. Twenty years, or maybe more—the precise time-lapse escaped him. So that's how long he'd been fighting the stairs, and it had seemed like a losing battle at that point, even though he had yet some strength in him to fight. The exact time when he recognized the stairs as his enemy didn't even matter; what did, though, was the fact that the struggle never relented but rather became more heated and violent. Was it always like that? Probably not; however, by then, he could hardly remember his life before the era with stairs had started…

Again and again, even after fleeting acquaintances had been replaced by a permanent, fully legitimate wife who would often join him on his frequent business trips, especially if he was heading to places that puzzled her or at least were yet to be visited by her, it was the stairs that spoiled the party. He recalled how she, a great appreciator of walking and climbing, had dragged him to the top of the fortress wall in Dubrovnik, with its countless ascents and descents. He had plodded behind her, loathing her legs. Those shapely things had flashed in his eyes, flying up and down the stairs with ease. She rushed him from one picturesque landscape to another. He would rather die than admit that his legs were not up to the task of climbing the next staircase, and so he, in order to get a tiny bit of rest, would stop as if to admire the view from above. He was not really looking at anything but regurgitating the only thought left in his head, *just how many more of these damned stairs would have to be counted before he would be able to plop down on a cool sheet in his hotel room?*

Extra pounds. Those extra pounds his wife would time and again chew him out over—yes, he had always been overweight, and it had never been a hindrance, or technically, had not been one (provided the trigger was extra pounds and not something less obvious and more infernal) until this feud with stairs began.

Never forgetting to count the steps, he piled issues upon issues in his mind. He remembered Sicily, where their hotel and conference hall stood upon the steep coast of the Mediterranean while all the better restaurants recommended by their concierge were down by the water. Sitting at the table laden with plates of the most amazing food and bottles of earthy Sicilian wine, he, like others, would give proper respect to the meal, but the frightening thought in his head would not go away. *After such a dinner, how was he supposed to keep up with his group while climbing all these hundred and thirty-four*—he still remembered the exact number—*steps back to his room?*

Or those tiny Italian towns where his partners would arrange business meetings so often and then offer to go on a stroll, always having to stroll up the stairs leading from the completely civilized foot of the hill, complete with comfortable hotels and decent restaurants, to the summit with the old downtown, which for some inexplicable reason would always seem fascinating and worthy of special attention to his colleagues, albeit those squares, churches, and magistrates of those innumerable Tuscan and Umbrian hills always looked identical. He would walk obediently and climb in despair, trying to stay out of the conversation and save the sheerest remaining bits of breath, cherishing the dream of going down the same stairs in an hour or two.

It was no better this time. Nobody had forced him to agree to celebrate the conclusion of their meeting at that fancy restaurant on the top of the mountain overlooking the city, even though there were plenty of equally fancy restaurants a stone's throw away from the hotel that could be reached without having to climb any stairs at all. He could name half a dozen of those, and as a patriarch, his opinion would have been heeded. But no, he agreed with them young billy goats that a dinner with a view of the night city would be the bee's knees, and it was there that they had to end their short but very fruitful visit to this place. Putting it straight, that was an ill-considered decision he made either to feel young together with them or to prevent them from feeling that he was not young anymore and now he labored over the steps of this endless staircase.

"Why am I even climbing here? I saw the map. It was entirely possible to take a detour over a few streets and get there in no hurry. Slowly but surely, over the not-so-steep pavement, saving myself these stairs-some palpitations and panting…Blast me; I wanted to save time! Take a shortcut up the stairs! Who could have known there would be no end to this staircase!"

Sixty-five, sixty-six, sixty-seven…

"Nah, rest is a must now, or I'll spit my heart out. I also need to catch my breath; something awful. I already suspected they were lying to me all the time. There's no way the air is twenty percent oxygen. Eight, maybe, and even that might be an overestimation."

He leaned against the railing and tried his best to breathe deeper and calmer, but still, his inhalations were jerky and shallow.

The evening lights of the city gleamed down below. What was so special about the evening lights? Lights are lights, nothing more, nothing less. He could not even make out what exactly was lit up down there. Why should this be considered some kind of a picturesque view? Okay, it would be nice to see the city during the day, when at least it could be seen properly, along with the river, the beautiful bridge, and the enormous pile of the cathedral, but what was there to be seen at night?

Propped up by the metal railing, he looked down, feeling other people passing him, those who apparently did not think much about climbing the stairs, judging by their quick, even steps.

He kept looking down, watching, or rather, feeling the birds that were flying between him and the city lights in the dark; their coming could only be registered through the momentary disappearance of certain light spots. For some reason, he recalled how, a long while ago—he had even forgotten the exact time and place—he had been looking out the window of his hotel room near the airport, recording the bright sea of beacons at the airfield, and had suddenly taken notice that some of the landing lights and illuminated hotel windows on the other side of the fence behind the port had been going out only to reappear very soon, and then the neighboring ones would do the same as if some dark tide had been slowly rolling down the strip. It had taken him some time to realize it had been just another airliner being pulled to the runway, its indistinguishable bulk passing between him and the lights.

This flashback pulled him even further back to one long-past fall when he had sat at home by the window, watching the fog come out of the forest into the clearing in front of his house. The fog, slow and inevitable, had blurred every tree diligently, leaving only a few dark spots, which then would also fade until disappearing into the white, and then the fog would take on the next tree...

He shrugged the apparition off, realizing all those memories were tricks pulled on him by his conniving memory to keep him in this place and delay his toilsome ascent as much as possible. No way. He was stronger than that, and he would continue his campaign upward. His time was short; no, short would be an understatement; he was already fifteen minutes late, so his fellow diners had probably already sat down to eat. He who hits the party last isn't typically worth the wait.

And he got a move on, accompanying his steps with a verse that felt quite appropriate at that point: *'We...can...stick...out...'unger, thirst, an' weariness, But...not...not...not...not the chronic sight of 'em.'* It helped him beat another thirty. And then this followed, becoming increasingly painful and intermittent.

Eighty-two...Eighty-three...Oof...Eighty-four...

His eye caught a book lying (abandoned? Forgotten?) on the steps, likely left by the university students, who, as a local explained to him, would stop on the stairs and use the daylight to go through their course manuals on their way from the lower to the upper campus. Then his memory threw him off again, and he recalled those large, rough, faded books with their thick brownish paper, ridden with tiny letters—the omnibuses containing complete works by classics of the past. It always seemed weird to him how something like a complete collection of Pushkin on his father's shelf, ten stout volumes bound in blue and gold, sure one can collect whatever you want in ten volumes, but it all could just as well be compressed into one book and again be called complete. Then somehow, those books disappeared after sitting for a while on the farthest, least attractive shelves of numerous used bookstores. He remembered those stores well. They enabled him to realize that books were not only good for reading but also for sticking them into the clerk's hands with a less-than-honest 'Mommy sent this', to be rewarded with a few crumpled bills and coins for fear and sweaty armpits.

Then he recalled something else, and yet something else, and then he didn't even know anymore what he was thinking about, but he went on climbing slowly and stubbornly, catching thorny chunks of air with his mouth and feeling the uneven heartbeat resound in his ears.

One hundred and eight...One hundred and nine...One hundred and ten...

Time felt frozen. Nobody was overtaking him anymore: it was late already, and there was no one on the stairs at the point where he reached the 110s, already late for the dinner, which he had forgotten anyway. All he remembered was another staircase he faced, having to climb it to get somewhere.

They were waiting for him upstairs. They waited for a long time, but half an hour had passed since the time of the appointment, and they chose to begin without him. Someone even uttered assertively, as if summing up the wait, "It seems as though he'd changed his mind. We won't see him."

And they would not indeed…

He was found in the morning when the janitors came out to clean the stairs and remove the last night's aftermath: coffee cups, beer cans, cigarette butts, and whatnot. He was kneeling down, his head leaning against the rocky wall on the right. No one could see him from below or above, as the mid-landing where he stopped was out of sight from pretty much any vantage point. Had someone cared to count, it would have turned out that this was the hundred and thirty-third step if counted from below, and there were still seventy-two more to go…

The Man in the Next Bed

...in the fate of almost every person, there is something tragic—only often this tragic is closed from the person by a vulgar surface lives...
Another lady complains that she has a bad stomach and doesn't know what to do. But really, she wants to say that her whole life broken...
I.S. Turgenev

The second bed was rolled into my room late in the evening when I was almost falling asleep, trying not to think about the reasons and consequences of what I was in this room for. It had actually had two beds before, but since the occupants of this ward were, by definition, short-lived-only for a short period, when they were wheeled in here for surgery from one of the main buildings to allow them to settle down and prepare for the operation and then rolled away to the next operating block; my previous neighbor was also wheeled away early in the morning, and his place, contrary to all my expectations, was empty until the evening and was filled only now. And so, I spent the whole day in sad solitude, wondering why I was being pickled in this temporary ward for the third day; two neighbors were replaced, and the doctors did not really explain anything. They don't even come in. Only a sweet little nurse with a warm smile in response to all my questions convinces me that everything is going according to plan and there is no need to worry. That's where you start to worry. So it's best to sleep if you can fall asleep. Even now, I hoped to fall asleep quickly because sleep, driven away by the soft rustle of the wheels of the imported bed and the footsteps of the paramedics pushing it, was ready to return, and the new neighbor, it seemed, was not going to make any noise. But here I was wrong. Sleep had not yet come when I heard a soft call from the next bed:

A neighbor, a neighbor! Are you still awake?

Since the hospital fraternity requires careful attention to others, in case they are even worse off than you, I had to answer:

"No, not yet. Just taking a nap."

"Well, then, so I didn't wake you up," the voice rejoiced. "When will they cut you? In the morning? What's the reason?"

The same unspoken protocol of hospital behavior did not allow such a question to be left unanswered.

"I don't know. They should have been the day before yesterday. Intestine. Yes, they are pulling something. I'm trying to sleep it over. The morning is wiser than the evening."

I tried to be brief, to let the new neighbor know that I was not in the mood for a long conversation, but the effort was in vain. Not in the sense that a long conversation, after all, took place, but in the fact that the neighbor did not intend to have a conversation, but he definitely wanted to talk himself. So my brief answer was a trigger for him to start talking, and my short "aha" and "uh-huh" were more than enough to confirm that he still had a listener and had not yet shut out his words with sleep.

"I have lungs. And all so fast. I've always felt great, and I still do. But about a month ago, I coughed, as usual, in the morning in the bathroom, and the taste of blood in my mouth. I spat—and there was a blood mark on the white earthenware. I thought—accidentally, I rinsed my throat with warm water for order, but still, I began to follow. And so, it went. I coughed a little, and the handkerchief was covered in blood. A week later, I went to the doctor. So, they say, and so. In one day, all the tests and X-rays scrolled, and groped me all and said that in the left lung, something stuck somewhere near the top. How so, I ask—I did not smoke; I was engaged in sports. It happens, they say, but you need to cut it as soon as possible, and then you may also need chemistry or radiation if it has spread. Chances are if they're not lying. Who can I trust now? That's where I ended up. Well, that's fast. And then they say that others have been waiting for weeks."

"Sometimes," I said.

But he didn't seem to hear.

"They told me I'd be the first one there tomorrow morning…I wish I could…You know, I'm kind of a tough guy, I haven't been afraid of much in my life, and I've been thinking about her all these days."

He was obviously trying not to say the word 'tumor', just some kind of 'she'.

"More precisely, not even about her, but about what will happen next. It's interesting when I was a boy and just a young one, I sometimes wondered, rarely though, how old people, especially seriously ill people, feel and what they think about death. You understand, I was sure that in old age, not only people themselves but also their thoughts somehow change so that death already seems normal and in any case, there is no such fear as in youth, before it. But now, I myself am already, one might say, an old man, and I do not feel any peace, so to speak, like a young man. The same fear as when I was young. Maybe it's because everything happened to me so quickly—just my brain didn't have time to prepare, huh? It seems that no. Doesn't matter how old I am, I understand now that this age only shell. And under it is the same kid and all the same fears, like a young man. That is, as it were, age only spoils our material side, but inside, we are still the same as in our younger years. Well, when we stopped being boys and realized ourselves at the age of, say, twenty-twenty-five. That's how we always remain inside. And the rest—wrinkles there or gray hair—it's just like that. Outside. Well, like an old book— the cover is faded, and the pages are yellowed and begin to break, but the content is still the same. Don't you?"

"I guess so," I said.

"And it turns out that what you were deprived of in your youth, with that, you approach the threshold. Of course, life compensates some people in the process, but this is rare. And in the norm—born to be, born to do. Here, for example, I have a life that seems to end soon, and there is nothing to remember."

"How's that?"

"Like this. Everyone knows about someone, well, about all sorts of celebrities. It doesn't matter if they are a football player or a movie actor. And the other one who is nothing of himself, but he has interesting acquaintances, the same, say, football players or movie actors, and he is on friendly terms with them. And for people like me, it's neither. I remember how once I got drunk with a neighbor—he was some kind of unrecognized artist. He drank without stopping. So I got acquainted with some actor through this very drunkenness, as in the song—a famous actor from Taganka theater. That's what I was proud of. I still remember it, you see. Does he remember me, I wonder? Yes, what is there to ask—does not remember, of course. Probably didn't pay any attention. Was showing off only how significant he is. So, it's a one-way game. Who will remember me? Well, family, children—so it is for everyone, well, almost everyone, family and children. And they remember, as long as you're around. And so, you leave, no one will notice, just like you weren't there. So someone slipped by on their own invisibility, and that's it...And when was it noticeable to become or meet noticeable people? We only survived, no time for any meetings...This is now, say, we live in our apartment. And as a boy, I grew up in such a communal apartment that I don't want to remember. I remember inviting a couple of my classmates, with whom I was friends, home for a cup of tea. My mother left something to eat in the kitchen. And as I looked at our kitchen, not with my own eyes—my own are used to it—but as her guests will see, it was already creepy. And now I still remember how I bent over the sink—it was a low bowl, cast-iron, with enamel, once white, but all turned brown. Especially the one next door was a rare brew, never rinsed the sink behind her plates—and I rubbed it, rubbed it with a rag, either with soda or with some kind of cleaning powder, I don't remember any more, so that at least a little whiteness would return, so that…So I remember myself; the boy bent over the sink and rubs it in circles and rubs it…rubs it…not until whiteness, but modicum cleaner it has become. The neighbors were surprised later. The boys didn't even look at her, though. They probably had the same thing at home. So they drank tea and chatted. I somehow moved away then, but now I remember…Why would that be? They say you remember your whole life before you die, isn't that right?"

"I don't know…They say…"

"And I generally remember this old kitchen for some reason often now. We had a table in the corner, and it was close to the window, so it was comfortable to sit there—I didn't bother anyone, but I could see everything. There wasn't much to see, but it was still interesting to see how the neighbors lived. And it was convenient to read—the light from the window. Not that I was such a bookish person, but when I was sitting and cracking corn in a jar—do you remember that Khrushchev's twenty-eight-kopeck jar?—or sausages, from which you cannot tear off the cellophane? My mother always left this for me when she went on business trips. And I always read a book about delicious and healthy food. There was once such a thing, huge, with pictures. I still remember all the pictures—there was such a gorgeous table with wine and fruit. Here you eat this corn, and you read yourself what awesome, say, sausages are and how they are made. What is the composition of each minced meat—there are so many different types of meat I could not imagine! Or about caviar. I still remember that there are grainy, pressed, and ovary, here! I didn't even see any caviar until I was twenty, but that time there was so much saliva in my mouth that this corn was already digested even before getting into my stomach.

"True, there was a place where I felt on par with everyone else, although celebrities also looked there. Remember, in the 60s, there were such automatic wineries all over Moscow? You have twenty kopecks in the slot, and you have eighty-seven grams of port wine from the tap—as I remember now…"

"And not eighty-three?—I also remembered these machines."

"Maybe somewhere eighty-three, but where I went—on the embankment, not far from the Tretyakov Gallery, eighty-seven was. And if you throw two twenty-kopecks, it's a hundred and seventy-five. And for a dime, you could take a chocolate candy—'Chamomile' or 'Cornflower', and sometimes a dried sandwich with a circle of sausage or a piece of curdled cheese. beauty. That's where equality was. Not even equality, but fraternity. Usually, everyone went there in the morning to get better. And everyone understood each other, and everyone sympathized with each other. I've seen a lot of people there. I didn't know everyone, but people always said who was who. Here, they say, look who's hanging out with us. There have been no such places for a long time. I would have come in now."

"You cannot enter the same river twice," I muttered.

My remark gave a new direction to his thoughts.

Yes, the river…I liked to relax on the water. Fishing, boating, and everything else…I wonder what water does to people. Promotes relationships. Just recently, I remembered how I once received a trade union ticket to a boarding house on the Oka river. Poor, of course, but I'm fine, and the water is nearby. And next to the Pioneers' camp. Here, I am on the grass with a counselor I met from somewhere in the country. Pretty. Such a romance we have gone—just creepy. Only further than touching no way. Married, she says, even though she likes me. I did this and that, but I got a complete no. We just walked around and hugged a little. Well, my vacation is over. We separated. I did leave her my phone number, though. And what do you think—about a year later, she calls. I, she says, am in Moscow on business, and in general, there are big changes in my life. I divorced my husband, as he drank black, and made it clear that she did not mind seeing me. I was still single at the time, and I run to meet her right away. We met, and I can't believe it— well, not that scary, but certainly nothing particularly cute. And what I just fell for then! Or it's the water that does it. When the river is lapping at your feet, and the ugly beauties seem, and? Well, I, of course, went to the café with her, so that without rudeness, and left saying goodbye. Here's the story. Why did I suddenly remember her? There were many better girls. Or maybe I was remembering Oka, and she was just there…

"Yes, in general, I remember different things lately. Probably, we have some kind of sensor inside, which feels that something is wrong with you long before it manifests itself, and you notice it. I mean, they say that towards the end, old memories come up, or rather, memories of the old ones. And that means that if you remember such things, then you are not far from the end, eh? Here, look—I'm not a big fan of reading. So that in school I passed or then sometimes. And as a child—we didn't have many books at home, but my father sometimes bought huge volumes in faded cloth covers and all the complete collections. I remember Nekrasov, Leskov, Pushkin, Turgenev. I was still surprised at the time—how this is a complete collection and all in one book. I saw the collection of Pushkin on the shelf in the school library. Ten—as I remember now, bricks. Here, it is complete. And here, in one book, is everything. But I read it occasionally. yes, I forgot about these books a long time ago. Moreover, when I grew up and needed pocket money, I handed over these volumes one by one to the book dealers—they did not notice at home. And then suddenly, some time ago, I wanted to look through these books again. Not these writers, but these books. You'll believe it—I even went to the old book stores. Only found Leskov. There are no more such books. No one needs them. Nobody sells them, nobody asks for them They looked at me like I was sick when I bought it. And after all, I didn't even read it later, but I just held it in my hands, and it's nice. Why would that be, eh?

"But who knows why something suddenly comes to mind…

"I understand that I'm thinking about these books or the girl from the Oka because it's not for fun if you can say so. This is some kind of protection. After all, I do not evoke these memories. They come as soon as I start thinking about what will happen to me tomorrow. Well, not exactly tomorrow, but in general. In the future, that's still left. If there's any left, of course. And such fear creeps into the head and immediately throws up these memories. It's like I'm leaving tomorrow's death in the past. And there I am, still young, and everything is ahead.

"That's right—I could not stand it—Memory goes away—death comes. It's like Tyutchev's—"but it's even more terrible for the soul to watch all the old memories die in it."

"Who, who? It doesn't matter. So I'm not the only one who thinks so. And if not one, then it means everything is correct. I just don't remember, but I shield myself from the terrible with them. I'm telling you—protection. The head knows best how to protect us. Maybe these are the memories that distinguish old people. When you're young, you still have nothing to protect yourself with. Therefore, you do not think about the terrible, and then such horror will cover, and there are still no memories to cover up…

"And the worst thing about life is to think about it. I mean, how I lived it. I read once in my childhood with a writer—I forgot his last name, but I remember the story he wrote about nature. So he had such a bird invented, all of itself mediocre, and the color is not white, not black and not bright, and the wings are not long and not short, and the beak is not straight, and not cross, and not curved, well, in a word, everything is mediocre. So, when she tried to fit in somewhere in nature, she didn't fit anywhere. Each lifestyle requires its own specialization—where the color is white, where the wings are long, where the tail is short, where the beak is curved, and there is no place for such an average! Here and such as I, mediocre, not that there was no place at all—there you will grab a worm, here you will bite the seeds, and you will survive, but no one will say; here is a clear falcon, or a cheerful finch, or a beautiful oriole, just even no one will notice how something mediocre flashed…It occurred to me that in order to be noticed, you need to stand out in one thing, and so if you have let's say ten positive qualities, but only a little of each, so again, no one will pay attention. I didn't say the word 'ten' by accident. For example, do you know who is the most famous decathlete in sports?"

"No, I don't remember…"

"That's what I'm saying. And ask who is the best pole vaulter. Immediately—Bubka! And in the long jumps? Beamon! Best swimmer? Phelps! Everyone knows. And there are no decathletes. I can't remember myself because they don't set any records in any sport, and what are the champions in terms of total points? So who cares about this amount of points? Give people a basement so that you either the highest jumper or the fastest runner or put them on the floor with a single blow. So it is with life. Even if you score decent points in the decathlon, no one will even look at you…"

It seems that the neighbor became too loud to speak, so they heard him in the corridor, and the nurse came into the room.

"Why are you talking so late at night," she said reproachfully—"you need to get a good night's sleep so that you can be strong tomorrow. Surgery, after all. Let me give you a little shot to help you sleep better."

"I don't need to," I said in a deliberately sleepy voice.

The nurse fidgeted a little by the neighbor's bed and soon came out.

"Hey, neighbor," he called softly now—"it's really time to go to bed. But it's scary to close your eyes. I once spent the night alone in an old house. It was windy. If you close your eyes, everything sounds: the shutters slam, the rafters groan, even the floorboards creak, as if someone is creeping up on you. Half the night, I lay in the dark and stared until I fell asleep. Here and here…"

He muttered something else under his breath and then fell silent. I fell asleep. When I woke up in the morning, his bed was gone. Taken away for surgery. In the afternoon, when the nurse brought me lunch, I asked her about the neighbor. "Yes, everything will be fine with him," she said. "The tumor was small and encapsulated, so most likely, there is no need to fear metastasis. He'll be discharged in three days."

And I was sent home the same day in the evening. They said that they decided not to do the surgery; somehow, it is difficult to get to her—I also do not call her by name—it is better to try chemistry. I've been trying it for a year now, and I'm still alive, but what's next? We'll see. Young memories are not catching me enough yet…Maybe it will be fine…

Death of a Man

This man was Nikolai Ivanovich, and as for his death, no one would have dared to predict it to Nikolai Ivanovich on the morning of that sad day. Things were bad enough for him—the second heart attack was no joke, but still, two months had passed, and after being discharged from the hospital, he had already been living at home for a week, waiting for a ticket to a sanatorium. And sixty-three is not the age to give up on your life even after two heart attacks. True, the doctors did not advise him to go out yet, although his house stood right on the edge of the park; no, not even a park, but a forest, the green—on the map—language of which crept insinuatingly into Moscow along the Yaroslavka road. That was why Nikolai Ivanovich spent these days sitting at the window, listening to the more and more steady and pain-free movement of his heart, which was getting used to normal work on the left side of his ribs. Looking down from the height of his eleventh floor at the shaggy layer of foliage below, the green clouds of which were being beaten by the dirty yellow of the city autumn right before his eyes, and imagining how in just five or six days, he would be quietly wandering through the alleys of the sanatorium he knew and recover with the help of crisp and bright gold of the September forest of Moscow suburbs.

That morning, however, Nikolai Ivanovich felt a little uneasy. No, his heart didn't hurt, and he didn't have shortness of breath, and he had an appetite for breakfast—he was getting up late now so his wife would leave him something from the convalescent menu on the stove in a covered frying pan, or right on the table under a pot set upside down, although, to be honest, he could already have made himself what he needed, since the refrigerator was full to the brim: in the week of his home life, his daughter and son had stopped by three times and brought an infinite number of bags and jars with something useful or simply tastier. No, that wasn't the point. It was just that almost two months in the hospital: two weeks lying down, two weeks with short trips to the corridor, and three more with prison-like walks in the pitted, ugly square near the hospital building and especially this endless week at home, when he could already observe the daily normal city bustle so closely, brought Nikolai Ivanovich, a man quite active and energetic in already so distant normal life, to complete insanity. As a well-bred man, Nikolai Ivanovich considered himself to be so, not without reason; he did not vent his irritation on his family; he was very gentle with his wife and affectionate with the children, but even in their presence, and especially when he was alone, there were some strange movements and longings inside him, so that he himself, a specialist in steam installations and generators, resembled a far from new boiler under obviously excessive pressure.

In the long time that had passed since the beginning of his illness, Nikolai Ivanovich, at least so it seemed to him, had managed, as it should be, to sort out his rather monotonous life in his head, to recall his parents, who were already long ago buried by him in German cemetery and regularly, once a month, visited by him; the first wife; a beautiful and clever woman, who, for absolutely incomprehensible and still unexplained reasons, linked her bright and busy life for several months with the monotonous existence of Nikolai Ivanovich, flashed by a few months in a single color, post war Moscow; in fact, she did not need a Moscow residence permit, and she earned a decent income, and there were more than enough fans around her, so that these incomprehensible few months remained the only unsolvable mystery in his transparent past; and the story of his subsequent and much more traditional affair with his second wife—the current one; and the few, if one may say so, pranks, which, however, did not leave any noticeable trace either in his life or in his memory, and usually associated with long business trips to places where they did not know how to install or use these very steam installations and generators with sufficient skill; and the birth of children, who were born in the most prosperous way, and did not give him much trouble with their growth or studies, and grew up so friendly, strong, intelligent, calm, decent and happy in family life. So, don't trust those who says that there are no such things our days, it still happens. And a few vacations on the Black Sea and much more numerous trips to the rented dacha near Moscow for a quarter of a century, and all sorts of family celebrations, relatives and friends, and even just acquaintances, well, and all that other stuff that Nikolai Ivanovich quite rightly considered his life. Oddly enough, memories and reflections that were not related to the family and what is commonly called the family circle came to his mind much less.

And it is not surprising at all—he was not released from the factory to fight in WW2 and almost fell into the deserters of the labor front when he too persistently began to ask for the army volunteering, sending letters and requests to those instances where he was not supposed to apply in any way. His further life in its classic three-stage; worker, master, engineer was connected with the same plant, which a few years ago, however, turned into an association, which, of course, did not lead to any changes, and with the same, well, almost the same colleagues who knew each other inside out. It involved the necessary amount of scandals and reconciliations, reprimands and thanks, business trips to the south and north—once even to Bulgaria, for which he still retained his gratitude to their then director, and even spoke once in his defense at a meeting where he was cursed for nothing by the factory superior that visited them. Or was it already an association? This deputy minister, who just had to take out the evil on someone, said that all these steam things produced by them are much worse than he saw in one distant foreign country, which the minister himself visited a week before. Well, in general, all that should be in the life of a smart and hard-working engineer who put his strength into the development of our native domestic industry. So if his parents, his wife and children, and even his dacha near Moscow were all his own, then the work was the same as that of many dozens of people who worked nearby, so to speak, belonged to everyone, and therefore it was impossible for Nikolai

Ivanovich to remember it, and everything connected with it in his critical circumstances, and let God be with all this.

So everything was weighed and calculated, and Nikolai Ivanovich was not particularly displeased—no worse or better than the others, and maybe even higher than average: the children were far too good. So, the reason for the longing was something else. Unclear from the very beginning, it gradually became more painful so that Nikolai Ivanovich suspected the return of his heart troubles, but the pulse taken on the carotid artery as the doctors in the hospital taught him, was smooth, without any interruptions, suspicious haste, or slowness that clouded his head, there was no pain in his chest, no shortness of breath, and if there was a shiver in his left hand, it was probably because he had been standing at the window for almost half an hour without noticing it, leaning on it and looking with unseeing eyes at the treetops and occasionally passing through gaps in the greenery of lonely passers-by below him.

But 'unseeing eyes' is a wrong term—they saw everything, and even if you don't seem to be looking at something on purpose, this uncertain something, and everything surrounding it, is inside you, and there a miracle happens—the outside world collides somewhere in the depths of your consciousness with its reflection thrown there by 'unseeing' eyes, so that out of this collision, the real one is finally born, which suddenly pops up in your head in its absolute clarity and completeness and remains there now forever, even if you close your eyes, turn away, or you'll fall asleep. This also happened to Nikolai Ivanovich—he suddenly regained his sight, and his now-seeing eyes turned down to the trees, the paths, and the people. He understood now why he had been pining and what he had missed, or rather what he had missed—this forest, these paths, these infrequent passers-by in the daytime. This world was empty without him, and here he was, just a double window-glass and eleven floors away from what was waiting for him.

Nikolai Ivanovich once again listened carefully to himself, thought a little about the doctors 'instructions, decided not to take them into his head, and carefully moved from his unbelted housecoat into his sports walking suit, which was only a little too big for him, after some thought, put on his coat in the corridor and left the apartment, resolutely and irrevocably slamming the black diamond-shaped pattern decorated leatherette door behind him.

There was no one in the elevator, and Nikolai Ivanovich enjoyed his complete independence. The unpleasant longing disappeared, replaced by an impatient excitement, which even responded with a few convulsive heartbeats, but Nikolai Ivanovich had already left the entrance; the trees were only a short distance away—twenty paces across a strip of constantly torn clay with the remnants of building concrete stuck in it like glacial boulders; his open mouth sucked air noisily into his lungs, his heart calmed down, another twenty unhurried steps—oh, how he wants to hurry, then another set, and then, turning around, Nikolai Ivanovich no longer sees his newly abandoned house behind the bushes. Nikolai Ivanovich stomped for a while in the small clearing, remembering his usual route, which had been pushed out of his memory by the fear-filled walks from the ward to the doctor's room, from the ward to the dining room, and then from the ward to the stunted park, and slowly moved along the empty path into the depths of the forest. In his memory, the doctor's advice from a week ago before he left—not to get tired, not to hurry, not to abuse, not…not…But it was no longer up to them, and Nikolai Ivanovich plodded on and on, on the ground, wet from the recent rain, which was so long waiting for him.

He did not notice the infrequent passers-by, but he felt their presence and was glad that they, too, had waited for him and that he had so confidently taken his rightful place among the people and trees. Nikolai Ivanovich did not know how long he was walking through the forest, did not pay attention to the twists and turns of his path, and only occasionally noticed suddenly the red spots of a rowan tree behind a low shrub on the side of the road, then an old pine tree with a forked lyre-shaped trunk, or an inappropriately bright empty cigarette pack thrown into the grass by a sloppy passer-by. And there was nothing on his mind.

Suddenly it seemed to him that it was already beginning to get dark, and the distant trees lost their independent appearance, merging into a flat yellow-green plane, along which he slowly glided towards the incoming wind. His left hand was slightly numb, probably from the cold, and he carefully put it in his coat pocket. The bushes close to the road drifted back, lingering for a photographic moment in the corners of his eyes, then disappeared completely. Nikolai Ivanovich felt hot. The wind made it difficult to walk, blowing his unbuttoned black coat behind him. The air became as thick as water, and for no reason at all, it seemed to Nikolai Ivanovich that he was drowning. It was so real that he beat his soft hands in the air, which flew in slippery chunks between his fingers. The swollen coat pulled down. He tried to throw it off, but it got tangled with the wind and kept his hands from getting free. Now it was the most important thing—to free his hands, and Nikolai Ivanovich, taking a deep breath so as not to choke, kept tearing and tearing out of his sleeves. At last, he felt himself free, the black rag disappearing into the stream, his movement becoming easier. A lazy thought told him that something was wrong, that it shouldn't be like this, but he couldn't figure out what it was, and he continued to float slowly in the leaf-streaked air from one vertical trunk to the next.

After a while, Nikolai Ivanovich felt pressed against the same lyre-like pine tree that had already met him on the way. He stood with both arms wrapped around the trunk and his head tucked into a small oblong hollow in the bark. Clarity of understanding returned to him, and with it, the numbness in his left arm, the growing pain in his chest, and the inability to fill his lungs with air, which was stuck somewhere in his throat and pushed deeper only in small pieces.

His head was spinning, and Nikolai Ivanovich began to reproach himself slowly and almost indifferently that he had not listened to the doctor and, without calculating his strength, had hurried to take his place in the normal world, which no one would have taken away from him anyway. He thought that if he moved from tree to tree, resting as long as he needed, he could get back to the his house entrance or just run into someone, and then they would take him back to the familiar hospital room and onto the bed to the left of the window, and again people there would do everything necessary for him so that he could sit in his dressing gown by the window and look down at the crowns of trees and people flashing in the park. He let go of the pine tree, took a few steps, and almost hung on to the smooth birch, the white trunk of which he took for a pillow in his fatigue, and pressed his forehead against it. Sweat poured down his face, down his back, down his legs, and he felt like he was drowning again. Nikolai Ivanovich suddenly sobbed but almost immediately calmed down. He remembered that not long ago—what was two months like—he was already dying, and he was thinking about his whole life, and saying goodbye to his wife, and thinking about how good his children were, and even something about steam boilers and generators, and how everything had gone no worse and no better than with the others, so now there was no need to think about all this again—after all, nothing has changed in these two months, and if nothing changes in two months, then what kind of life is it, even if you are sixty three and so you can drop the trunk and swim while you still can.

Nikolai Ivanovich did so. His body grew heavy, and he began to sink quickly into the cold and shivering air, and the frightened leaves shied away from him and then gathered in yellow flocks and watched something large and dark sink to the bottom.

And the waters closed over him.

After

...and the herd of dead is sad...
The dead are mostly docile...They love
the peace...for them, the memories
mean more than conversation...
—I. Annensky, *Laodamia*

At first, after my death, I preferred solitude. First of all, in my last days, there were far too many people around me, well, doctors, nurses or nannies (everything happened as it should, in a hospital, with the help of all the necessary achievements of medicine). I don't even count them, although no—I would be happy not to count them, but you cannot get away from them. They also do their job, as they understand it, so as a doctor's detour—they deceive, comfort; they come to make injection—again deceive and calm down. The hospital duck, finally, is brought out, and even then, they will say something warm or will hint at God (it is for my own money, after all, it doesn't matter that it is my wife who pays them for this duck—hers means mine). So there is no opportunity to focus on the upcoming event, though the need to focus is necessary; I felt it, and I remember it exactly. And I also felt that there was almost no time left; the last of it is going away, but they keep on distracting you.

And the neighbors in the ward? Well, okay, they will say that there was only one neighbor, but only for the last three days, and before that, don't you want eight? What would you say about eight of them? And this last one, even if he was silent all the time, I still felt him next to me, and there were no fewer doctors around him, so my attention was distracted and distracted. Even in normal life, I could do something serious—think, for example, only in solitude—and here, in addition, there was such a nasty smell of competition: *who was ahead, him or me?* So that as soon as he got silent, to the point of complete inaudibility, I was no longer focused on my own thoughts, waiting to see who would run up to him. If it's the entire team on duty, this means it goes to the end, or if there is only a nurse with a syringe, this means some small filth on the monitor screen slipped by. Again, there is no peace.

And the kin? My God, well, while I was healthy and not here, they rarely wanted to see me—not all of them, of course; I often saw many of them, I mean the distant ones. Anyway, you can't see enough of somebody before he dies; better look at my photos piled up at home. I can give everyone a pack, and my wife will still have another for every day of her life, and besides, I look much better in them, so no…As soon as I saw my aunt four days before, who only congratulated me on the round anniversaries and even then only on the phone, I immediately realized that it was the time…I just mumbled something kind to her (since that's the appropriate thing to do, please have it), and then, as it should be, the wife, children, a sister with her husband, a ten-year-old niece, *why did they bring her?* I understand, of course, she achieved it by throwing a tantrum, but when would there be another chance to look at her uncle, who is about to die? Even then, she was told not to show him her knowledge; you could see how interesting it is for her and scary to the point of horror, and how she wants to touch me, what I am like dying, although just a month ago you couldn't get her to sit on your knees, and above dropper like in the movies. If only she would not forget all this to tell her girlfriends in the neighborhood. My sister spoils her, after all. In general, there has never been so much chaos and fuss around a person as when the curtain is falling.

And all this is for nothing. He (or I, anyway) is already halfway there, and it's the perfect time to think about how and what, but when is there time to think? At night? No, even though all of this is about to end, at night, I still want to sleep, and it's better to sleep, and even then, there are nighttime thoughts; no matter how you look at them, they are confusing and are often not about what you want; any rustle leads them in the wrong direction. And there is none of the wanted peace put into them. So after all that happened, being alone, just being alone, and nothing else, I needed it.

Secondly, and also quite naturally, I wanted, since I could not before, at least post factum, to remember, arrange, analyze, measure, count, and weigh, to think about what is now and what will happen in the end. Although, of course, what will happen next—wherever I end up, I am stuck there. One could, of course, first try to somehow adapt to this new form of self-awareness (I almost said 'existence' out of old memory), setting aside all of these calculations that are of purely academic interest for later. Fortunately, 'later' in this context does not have any marked boundaries, although, on the other hand, I have already managed to understand that even here, it is tacitly assumed that somewhere, well, let's say, ahead, there must be a new boundary, as sharply marked as the one that we have all already crossed, but what is beyond that border, is again known as little as it was known to me, and all of us about what was waiting here. There are all sorts of theories on this subject, but I am not accustomed to reasoning without sufficient grounds, and my natural skepticism, which seems to have suffered little during my transition, does not allow me to be satisfied with something like 'the Formidable Judge'.

In general, no one would consider it cowardice (although no one cares and no one would even ask what I think about this) if I was in no hurry to remember and ponder it. There are few, however, who, with long…*what, I wonder?* God knows what measurements to use here; I haven't learned that yet, or maybe it's impossible to learn it at all. Well, just not having thoughts about what was back there: some from indifference, some from fear, and some from conviction—why when nothing can be changed anyway, and so the bad will always elicit shame, there will be eternal grieve for good, and you can go from shame to sorrow and back again forever. It was easier for Sisyphus— all there is to do is get started. There are also those such as this; however few, and nobody likes them and are even afraid of them. *Oh, how not to be infected.* After all, memories do not disappear and do not age here; what you came with is what you are sentenced to be with. There is only one way out—not to think about it at all, especially since here, if you decide not to think about something, you do not think about it, and such thoughts do not even arise inadvertently until you call them out yourself.

Here, too, some protection is triggered; as soon as you find yourself on this side, something new immediately appears, or rather, the old disappears—the pull to go back. Of course, I can only say this with confidence for myself, but it seems that others have the same feeling, and only a few look into the past that really what has passed has passed! Only these pestilent ones remain. It's much easier to lure something nice and non-essential out of the surviving experience and spin around it, spin, spin…and it doesn't get annoying.

But now, I understand this better; after all, I decided to think about what happened again, and only after that, keeping in mind the results of my calculations and reflections, to get used to the new present. What is good here—this is how quickly you begin to find joy in a new situation—is that residing in a slightly iridescent pinkish-gray fog, with the effort of thought so weak that you even feel it only after it is done and its results are already around you, you can immediately find yourself in that internally, apparently, absolutely mirage-like, but externally, equivalently, absolutely real environment, which based on the impression of your former life, most of all suits your momentary mood.

I liked to be alone on a small gray bench with a rusty nail protruding from the right side, between two crooked birches on the tall and deserted shore of a forest lake, for it was this bench, these birches, the shore, and the lake where it once happened upon me to spend about fifteen minutes.

When I was still vacationing there in a small bed-and-breakfast nearby, that later, unbeknownst to me, began to live in me as a standard place for solitary reflection. There I placed myself in the hope of finally collecting my thoughts, namely important and significant thoughts, and finishing thinking out all the unfinished thoughts from the pre-departure chaos. But the strange thing is that a flat gray surface with short, slightly grayer longitudinal strips of nonexistent—rather nonexistent here but quite real somewhere out there—water that once also did not exist in that place, but then it became and now stands as if it always was and always will be, a dark green continuous strip of barely recognizable forest on the far bank ahead, so very distant that it seems almost invisible even in memory, a trick of the light, an optical illusion on the border between the gray water and an equally gray sky, except that the colors are more uneven and lighter from the sun hidden behind low clouds (I don't like the bright light here, just as I didn't like it there), an incredible silence, in which I could not, by any effort, summon any sound from anything alive; not the splashing of an occasional fish, not the late-afternoon cheep of invisible birds in the branches of two birches above me, not even the buzzing of once-hated mosquitoes, but only a steady and indefatigable rustle, so steady and so indefatigable that I soon refused to attribute it to the leaves of the frail trees on either side, rather, it was a sounding symbol of the rustle of leaves in general—all this took possession of me, took me away, scattered me, dissolved me, not allowing even a trace of contemplation to linger in my fascinated attention, not even a hint of thinking about something more significant than the gray water, the green strip, and the iridescent clouds. And if I closed my nonexistent eyes, such eerie darkness would enter me that, in fear of losing myself in it forever, I would once again summon from God knows where my reserved bench so that I could see and see the water, forest, and clouds. But the more I looked at them, the further away went such a rash, childish, frivolous, and, most importantly, unnecessary desire to remember, reason, and weigh.

And as I swayed in harmony with a shallow wave, whispering somewhere in the infinite depths under my feet, on my little bench that had come out of a rotten tree and was barely holding on by a rusty nail, I realized why everyone here had such wide-open and unblinking eyes on faces that were not really there, and why these eyes look, look, and look into some invisible distance, invisible to others, in which everyone has their own swaying water, their own clouds stand, and their own birds do not sing.

And I realized that this was really the end.

Winter Boots

As often, we sat in front of Sasha's TV that evening and sipped a beer, looking, or rather, almost not looking, at the screen where real men were fighting on the ice. So, a tribute to tradition. And not to talk too much. After so many years of friendship, we no longer had to talk to each other to feel close. It looked like Sasha even closed his eyes. I focused on the beer. His wife, as always, was busy in the kitchen—even if I was such a frequent guest, not even a guest, but almost a member of the family, she considered it her sacred duty to feed something delicious, for which she is a great inventor and master. So the smells were magical to us.

Here on the threshold appeared Sasha's offspring—a young twenty-year-old miracle named Igor.

"Father, Uncle Kolya (it's me)—I came to say goodbye."

"Well, where are you soaped up in such a refined form, son," asked Sasha.

I must say that the child really looked exceptionally solid-in a dark three-piece with a tie and shining brown shoes.

"Yes, today the management is giving a reception in honor of the acquisition of some European company and asks us to look formal. You can't miss it."

Igor had only recently been hired by a solid financial company and still treated his work and non-work duties with all the seriousness of a neophyte.

"Good!" With visible pride, stated the father. "And the shoes are so simply chic!"

"Well, chic—" Igor did not agree—"the most ordinary Clarks, and not even too expensive. Not some Lobb or Berluti. I live sparingly. But they look quite decent. Okay, I'll take my leave."

Igor went out. Sashka stared after him for a few moments. Then his face grew sad and hazy, and he reached back blindly to the beer table, groping for another bottle.

The Countess, with a changed face, runs to the pond. I commented—"What's happened to you all of a sudden?"

Sasha was silent for a while and then said sadly—"No, you can imagine-Clarks, Lobb, Berlusconi, that is, this Berluti! I don't know the words even now, and at his age, it was only the Skorokhod and the Paris Commune…And they all take it as given."

"Well, what do you want? Times change, and people change with them, not like our post-war generation. And he earns money, too, and he doesn't beg his parents thanks God!"

"Yes, of course." And Sasha was even more sad.

"Why did those shoes have such an effect on you, after all? Even if it's Clarks, who you don't know."

Sashka was still silent.

"You know, now I suddenly remember. And I didn't even think that it was stored somewhere in my head. And when I looked at the shoes—it was right there. It was like yesterday or even this morning. I told you, my father didn't live long after the war. Exactly as I read someone else, I don't remember—"We will not die of old age; we will die of old wounds." And he died of old wounds. So my mother pulled me and my younger brother alone. As I understand it now, she tore her navel just so that we would have everything like people—dressed, shod, fed. We hardly ever saw her at home—from one job to another. She only left notes—what to warm up for lunch and what to cook for dinner. Except when we had to update our wardrobe—and we were both growing up fast, so we didn't even have time to tear one down, and we already had to buy another—then she would take a Sunday shopping trip. Here and then— winter is on the nose, and it turned out that my last year's winter boots no longer fit on my foot—my foot grew over the summer. Well, my shoes will suit the youngest, but I still need the new ones. So it's time to go to the shoe store. And here's the thing: the guys from the class and I were standing at the entrance the night before, chatting as usual, and Anton Ivanovich shuffles past us from the next entrance. He came back from the war shell-shocked and slightly out of his mind. A little something—throws itself at people. We called him 'Anton Ivanovich is angry' as in the movie—very old movie. Well, here he shuffles, and he's already wearing winter boots—ugly ones, some kind of felt, fastened to the overshoe with a button. We waited until he was out of earshot, and then we started laughing at what a mess he was wearing. It was an old man's nightmare, even though he wasn't old yet, more like the fathers of those who still had them. Well, they giggled, giggled, then started talking about something else. But I could still see those shoes. "Farewell to youth," they were also called. How can you produce such shit—at that time, such a question did not come into my head, but how can you voluntarily put such shit on yourself. And when my mother took me to the store, I just thought that these shoes would not turn up. Well, as you can imagine, they were the ones who occupied the whole shelf. And their price, as I remember now, was nine rubles a pair. Mom immediately grabbed them."

"Look, son," she said, "good for winter and warm, and the price is good. Let's try it on."

"Well, I sat down, like a condemned man, on a bench to try on. I tried it on. Just even a little free-for-growth means."

"That's good," my mother smiles, "so we take it, and the issue is resolved."

"And I sit there, and I can't look up from the floor, and I can't say a word. Can't she see how ugly it is? And how the guys in the classroom and in the yard will laugh at me. And I'm in my fifteenth year—how the mockery feels then! So I'm silent and swallow my tears."

"Well, why did you hang your head," I hear my mother's voice, "Do you not like it, or what?"

"*Really*, I think she saw for herself how terrible and how old-fashioned. I look up to confirm that I will not wear these shoes for anything, and I see how my mother looks at me with pity and tries to smile, but it does not turn out to be her own smile."

"Okay, let's see how much more we can add to find something better," and he reaches into his bag.

"And what is there to climb something? Last night, when she asked me to bring her notebook out of her bag, I saw that the only thing in the open purse was two fives, a three-ruble note, and a ruble—just enough to buy bread, butter, milk, and two packs of dumplings for our Sunday family dinner.

"And suddenly, in spite of myself, I say something completely different from what I wanted—Oh, come on, Mom, these are great shoes, and they're just right for me, and they're warm. We take it, of course.

"I see that my mother has tears in her eyes, but she smiles again. And now—for real. She pressed the head of me sitting down to her stomach and did not let go for a good minute. Probably so that I wouldn't see her tears. So we bought it."

"Well, did the guys laugh?" I asked, just to say something.

"No, not really. Maybe they joked about it for a day or two, it didn't even ring out, and then it went away. And I still wore them for two or even three years—the leg almost did not grow anymore. So I felt like a real adult man after giving away just a little blood. More precisely, I did not really understand how exactly I felt, but I knew that I had done the right thing. Like this."

"And well done," I say—"Just what happened, it was. And cut it off. And you have a good boy even if he knows about Lobb."

Good one…Good…

Sasha paused again.

"I'm sorry for Mom."

The Spider

He had never been particularly fond of music. That is, he listened, of course, if it turned up-in the car there, when the road was long, he always turned on the 'Mayak' station while there was still a 'Mayak' doesn't matter if it was a symphony, or a bandstand, or folk music, still it was always more fun to go; at a party, when the dancing started, why not to swing, and it sounds quite pleasant; a couple of times a year even went to concerts, well, this is so as not to offend a friend, who is either the second or third violin—what do they count there?—he worked in the same orchestra that was performing, and he always invited him—you can't say no to that; that's all, I guess. And then—it rings, buzzes, strums, a crowd of people all around at these concerts, and you listen, listen, even if something comes to mind, so, some kind of porridge from the day you lived, the day after, and vague thoughts that you should somehow tune in to the right mood and imagine something more appropriate to the moment, and who knows what, in fact, you should imagine. Once, at the invitation of the same friend, he listened to a piece—he remembered the name because it sounded so very strange. "Afternoon rest of the faun," so what would you imagine if he had never heard of any faun! So, try to imagine who knows what, and how this who knows what is resting in the afternoon. From what, one wonders? No, what's not for him is not for him. You can't all like the same thing or think what would happen if all the men ran after one girl. A nightmare! Stampede!

And at that time, somehow by chance, everything slipped through: well, a business trip, well, they finish everything early, well, there was nothing to do in the evening a few hours before departure—he was in this city for the first time, and there were no acquaintances. He could, in the end, just stagger around the center and get some air for the road. Or go to the bar. Also, before departure, not bad. But a colleague of his, with whom he, in fact, did all the business, offered in the evening to go to the cathedral of the city—well, yes, it was once a cathedral, and now, as it should be, there is a café in the colonnade outside, and inside there is a museum and a concert hall; to go to an organ concert, and the organ, they say, is famous all over Europe, and the sound is some unusual; even some acoustics came to measure something there, and the program is unusual, and what's more—then a world celebrity is on tour—there are only three concerts in the city, and, most importantly, this colleague is connected with the musical circles, so they are provided with two seats upstairs in the choir, where you can look at the organist, this is just an extraordinary privilege because everyone who sits below can only listen, and who plays, they cannot even really see, this is not a concert for the piano with an orchestra where everyone only looks at the guy in a tailcoat on the stage. So he went and just had time to drop by the room to change his shirt and put on a tie—after all, an outing.

Well, in general, they came as expected. The interior is beautiful, of course; the various stained-glass windows, dark wood, carved benches, columns with sculptures, and the organ is barely visible at the top. He started to count the pipes but lost his way—the small ones were almost invisible from below, and besides, one column got in the way, then another, so he gave up. They wandered around the hall, but the people kept arriving—a full house, to be sure! So they decided not to linger any longer in the crowd below but to make their way upstairs. It was only from below that it seemed that the organ was not so high above, but when it was necessary to climb up this twisted tower staircase inside the gray stone, he was sweating all over before they got there. At the top, the organ was really huge (he decided to again count the pipes later when the concert start), and the thick pipes with holes went straight into the roof, glowing in the gathering gloom like well-oiled rifle barrels. On a tiny spot at the foot of the organ, in front of a complex machine with a keyboard and numerous pedals, there was a small chair lit by a dark yellow light, squeezed from all sides by tall wooden chairs with carved triangular backs that had been dragged up a narrow stone staircase (then he realized that they had probably been dragged here on ropes directly from below). There were twelve of these chairs (he chuckled tactlessly as he counted them), and two were assigned to them. There were no numbers on the seats, but they took the best, as they decided, of the remaining—six people were already sitting there. The others quickly filled up as well. A woman's voice spoke from nowhere through the speakers below. There was a burst of applause from the floor: apparently, the audience was hurrying with the beginning. Almost immediately, the same pleasant female voice—from whence he never understood—said something long in a local language he didn't know, probably the name and titles of the performer and the concert program, and then there was another clap from below. The musical aristocracy that surrounded them, to whose level they had risen thanks to the connections of his colleague, also moved their hands slightly, and right in front of them, in a yellow circle, an invisible from below performer appeared.

It was a good thing the floor couldn't see him, he thought, because a dozen people could still hold back their laughter, and out of a thousand people sitting below, someone would have laughed out loud, so out of place was the celebrity's appearance with the exalted music. A small, fat man in black, whose short legs and plump-fingered hands were absurdly protruding from his round body, was fidgeting on the chair, adjusting himself more comfortably to the console. It seemed that he could not stretch himself enough to reach all the necessary keys, pedals, and levers at the same time, but somehow he twisted, stuck his limbs to the required points, paused for a moment, and finally extracted the first low and vibrating sound from the tubular pile of metal (like a spider on a central heating battery, he thought).

The organ had always seemed boring to him, so he did not even listen to the music very much, having credited himself with the very fact of being in such an elegant place, and immediately began to count the number of organ trunks planned earlier. He decided to move from bottom to top and from left to right, marking the dozens with his curled fingers. At first, it was all right, though there was a buzzing and clanging all around; after he counted fifty, he couldn't get over it, and something he couldn't tell what—prevented him. He started again, got lost again, then again, and again with the same result, and then he realized how distracting, moreover, how exciting his attention was, the absurd black figure beating somewhere in the lowest corner of his right eye. He moved his eyes across the six bodies that were frozen in respectful and understanding attention and fixed his gaze on the twitching back of the organist.

Probably, from the point of view of a fly, this is called getting into the web. The spider felt the touch of his gaze on its back and, without looking, but without missing, threw the first thick and low humming thread in its direction. He jerked, but it was too late: outwardly disorderly, but in fact, in absolute harmony, known and audible only to the spider itself, the black body continued to twitch, contract, stretch, grow far beyond the yellow circle of light and again shrink to a barely noticeable cherry on the round leather chair, and with each movement threw out more and more threads in his direction, winding, enveloping, immobilizing him on the hard wooden seat designed to be a trap for such he needs insects. He still tried to move, to buzz, and to beat his wings, in the vain hope of breaking the flexible, glittering, and deadly-strong cocoon that was being erected around him, woven of thin threads as thin as a mosquito's squeak, held together with medium-thick threads made of the voice of the woman he loved, and finally sealed with thick ropes from the roar of the eight-point surf, but in vain…He was caught dead, and the cold terror of death rapture trickled down his back in thin trickles of sweat, bursting from the depths of his body through the instantly bulging volcanoes of enervating shivering, and closed his eyes with impenetrable curtains of eyelids so that no external action could tear his soul from the dizzying swaying on the web stretched throughout the huge hall. He had once read of a girl from the century before last who refused to believe in the deadly cruelty of natural harmony and believed that spiders served as nannies for flies and only rocked tired and fussy flyers on selflessly woven hammocks. And it was true, just as it was true that the spider-nurse, seemingly oblivious to her next charge, continued to move him slowly on the endless elastic wave, turning the swaddled carcass more comfortably so that with unerring touches, she could suck out his life and soul and absorb them into her body, which had swollen to the full light, ceiling, and sky…

He didn't hear the audience applauding, the next play being announced, his neighbors talking approvingly in short pauses, a worried colleague asking if he was all right and if he wanted to go outside because it was really stuffy here, he didn't see the light turn on, the round figure detach itself from the chair and the remote control, how it bowed to nothing, passing its pink sausage fingers over the exhausted keyboard with a farewell gesture the organ…On a carved brown chair lay his dry, empty skin, which took endless seconds to fill up again with the sounds, feelings, and sensations of the day.

He did not remember the name of the spider, nor did the name of the music he was playing, announced in a foreign language—they had not bought a program, there was no time to talk after the concert, and he was already flying away in the night—but he would recognize both the plump figure and the intertwined network of sounds, once he sees them again and he hears them, which is why he now often goes to concerts in the hope of feeling the sweet chill of immobilizing delight on his back again, so far in vain. That is, he likes it; it even seems to him that he has begun to understand something, but it still is not that…He needs a spider…The wife, however, is happy—much better than hanging out with his friends in the evenings who knows where…

At Night

Back then, they had only recently bought their house by the ocean. Although this, of course, is strong wording, 'by the ocean'. That is, the ocean, of course, is there, and to the place on the road where you can already see the water, really visible, a large space, not some kind of gap between houses, it is only fifty meters, and from that place to the water itself, the walk is only ten minutes at an average speed, no more, but still not right on the shore. Not at the water's edge. On the other hand, it would be twice as expensive, and such houses were not often on the market. But still, their entire village was considered to be located on the shore and by the ocean, so that means their home is also on the shore and by the ocean…

Well, that's not the point. There was just so much hassle with this purchase that they were completely swamped for a good three months. First of all, the house was not very new, so some repairs were needed. On the first floor, replace the floor, then paint the ceiling, then redo the toilet, then do something else. And on the second, although it was in better condition, some adjustments were also needed. Then the furniture was bought and arranged, then all the kitchen equipment, then the different TVs. And furthermore, every little thing required a trip from the city. Then the builders have some questions, then yet another sofa is delivered, then the master comes to check the electricity and put in new sockets, then something else…And they were so busy that there was no time to wander around the neighborhood—every time they finished with yet another job, had a quick snack, and went to bed sooner so that they could be in the city for work in the morning. And they slept, of course, like the dead.

That night, for the first time, was free. No repairs, no deliveries, no electricians. They just came to clean up a bit, take their time to have dinner, and finally enjoy their new home to the fullest. And they got it—they wandered through all the rooms, blew away dust mites, had dinner by the fireplace, watched some concert on TV, even read a little before going to bed, then went to sleep as normal people, and not as overworked horses, should. Beauty…

She woke him up at about two in the morning.

"Listen, I can hear something humming, but what exactly it is, I cannot understand!"

He opened his eyes, tried to wake up properly, and listened. At first, he didn't hear anything unusual—just the wind outside the window…However, after a few seconds, he indeed heard a low, measured hum from somewhere; it seemed to come from the very depths of the house.

"It's really buzzing," he said in surprise, already fully awake. "Do you remember if we turned the TV off?"

"We turned it off, turned it off," she said hurriedly. "I even pulled the plug from the socket just in case. It's something else…"

"Well, what else is there? Air conditioning and a water pump," he mused. "Maybe we left the water running somewhere when we checked the taps yesterday?"

"No, we didn't," she said impatiently and even a little frightened. "I checked everything again myself in the evening when you were still in the bathroom. Nothing was flowing anywhere. And we didn't turn on the air conditioner. Why do we need it now? Just open the balcony door…"

Their voices sounded faint and lonesome in the darkness.

"Listen, can't this be general heating? There's always something on, even if the air conditioner doesn't work. The master explained it to us. What if something broke there…can it start a fire?"

She was always afraid of fires, so he hurried to calm her down.

"It can't. After all, the same master said that there is some kind of reliable lock there. If something is wrong, it immediately cuts off the entire system, and the alarm starts to beep. And here, nothing is beeping. Let's listen for another minute; if we don't figure it out, I'll go look around the whole house…"

"I'll come with you!" She was obviously afraid and didn't want to be alone in the bedroom.

They fell silent and listened. And all at once, the whole night was filled with a hum that seemed to grow stronger as they talked.

"I'm afraid," she whispered, clinging to him. "Something is going to happen to the house. This is something bad buzzing…."

"Don't be silly; what can be bad here? The appliances don't work, and ghosts do not exist. Something is humming that should be humming. Probably some kind of transformer."

"No, transformers don't hum like that. They hum steadily. But here, listen, it grows stronger then quieter like a living thing...."

Indeed, there was a kind of uniform unevenness in the hum, like breathing, but whose breathing could it be?

"Wait, let me just get up and listen, standing up. I won't go anywhere yet, don't be afraid. Maybe I'll figure out what's going on."

He climbed out of bed, stood up, and took a few steps toward the balcony door, invisible in the nighttime. The hum seemed to grow louder as he approached the balcony. He drew back the heavy curtain as if spellbound and looked out of the room. The hum, which was now clearly outside the house, was waiting for just this to fill the entire space around it and even drown out the sound of the wind and the rustling of the swaying branches in the courtyard...She even screamed. But he already understood...

"Listen," he said in shock. "It's the ocean! It's the ocean humming!"

"What ocean?"

"Namely, this one! Ours, which beats against grim cliffs!"

"What are you talking about?" she said, a little more calmly, but was still incredulous. "It is far over there..."

"But look at it! What's your 'over there' to him if he lies in three directions for a thousand kilometers!"

"I'm coming to you!"

She got up too and joined him on the balcony.

They stood and listened dazedly to the voice of the ocean, languishing from the enormity of it.

"It's still kind of strange," she said timidly as if she was afraid the ocean might hear her. "When you're standing near the water, it sounds very different, even when there are waves…First stronger, then weaker, now rolling in, now rolling back, and you can hear it all so clearly…But here, somehow, almost evenly, just a little up and down…Why is that, huh?"

"Because when you're standing by the water, that's the only place you can hear it that uneven way. There, it turns out very distinctly. The wave will roll, then roll back. But here, you hear it from the whole coast at once, and the waves roll to different places with a slight shift in time, hence the uniform hum. Well, or with small overflows. Do you understand?"

"I understand…Why haven't we heard it before?"

"Because in the daytime, it is clear. There are so many noises around that it's not like the ocean. A grenade can explode, and you won't hear it every time. But at night…and what nights we've had all this time, we've been so busy and tired that a bomb could go off next to us and we wouldn't wake up…And when for the first time we went to bed as normal people, he showed himself…."

"How beautiful he sounds."

"Well, there it is, and you were afraid…Now just imagine how it sounds to those in the front row who live right by the water. No conservatories are needed. Lie down and listen…"

"Never mind that I have enough of it here. I'll lie and listen, too. Let's go back."

They lay down, this time without drawing the curtain all the way back to allow the hum to enter the room. There were no more fears, and the sound of the surf was…

"Unbelievable, ocean!" she murmured with delight.

And immediately fell asleep.

And he followed.

Darkness

Of course, when you hear that sugar used to be sweeter, young people were more well-mannered, winter was colder, and summer was hotter, then you can be quite skeptical about such a statement. Who can tell for sure? And not everyone thinks so, even if they sometimes say something like that. But what no one can doubt is that the darkness used to be much darker. Remember at least your childhood (I appeal to those who are over fifty). As a child, you would go to bed; your mother would pull down the heavy curtains or close the shutters, close the door to the corridor or the dining room—depending with what room was the bedroom connected, and you would find yourself in absolute darkness. That is, in such a way that even if you close your eyes, even if you keep them open, there is no difference. Except that with your eyes closed, it was much more frightening—although it was clear that even with your eyes open, you would not see any monster approaching your face from this darkness, but still the eyes opened and staring into the darkness gave you a ghostly hope that suddenly, after all, you would see and somehow manage to hide or dodge. But with the eyes closed—there was no chance of escape. And no matter how long you had to lie there and stare, you still didn't even see any outlines in the dark—your eyes didn't get used to it, and how can you get used to complete darkness? In addition, because of the absence of any visual stimuli, your hearing became impossibly sharp, and from every corner, and especially from under the bed, some rustles, creaks, and sighs began to creep into your ears so that it seemed that the enemy was approaching from all sides and there was no escape! All you had to do was yell in horror: "Mama!" and when your mother, alarmed by your cry, opened the door, through which a saving light instantly burst in, paving a yellow path from the door to your bed and driving the monsters that were approaching into complete nowhere, then you began to beg piteously to leave at least a small crack, at least a tiny strip of light, into which you could cling with your eyes and forget the rustles, creaks, and terrible inhabitants of the darkness, and then even close your eyes and sleep, sleep, sleep…But this, of course, if your mother could sympathize and regret or at least remember her once-present fears in the dark, but if she was oblivious or fearless and even wanted to raise a strong-minded man out of you (I can't say for the girls, because I don't know, maybe it was easier for them), then after a kiss on the forehead and parting words: "Do not be afraid and do not shout, you are no longer small, and you are a man!" the door would close tightly again, the saving ray would disappear, and you would once again found yourself alone against the solid darkness and everything that inhabited it…And you saved yourself as best you could, knowing now that there was no hope for your mother and the crack in the door—pulling the blanket over your head, or hiding your head under the pillow, or even sitting up in bed—for some reason, sitting seemed safer than lying down—probably in the hope that it would be easier and faster to get up and run (no matter where and from whom—the main thing is out of the dark and into the light!), than from a completely horizontal position, until you were completely tired, and sleep overtook you in the midst of it your fears. What a darkness it was! To all the darkness, the darkness is real, without fools.

It's not like that now. If at night I go into my bedroom, where the shutters are closed, and the heavy curtains are drawn, and close the door to the dining room, where it is also dark, then I find myself not in total darkness as I once did, but surrounded by many colored lights, although weak each by itself, but together giving enough light to accurately find the way to the bed, undress, and fold, without missing, the removed clothes on the chair by the bed, and pull back the blanket, taking exactly the corner of it, and don't hit your head past the pillow. And when you are already lying down, these lights are still with you and even suggest some thoughts…That faint yellow light in the distance is a lighted light switch, so that you don't have to fumble with your hand on the wall if you need to leave the room at night, but know that it is this light that you need to press to light the lamp under the ceiling. Then you immediately remember that, in fact, there is not one lamp in the sub-ceiling lamp, but three, but just one burned out, and that's almost a week ago, and you forget to replace it during the day's troubles, so you need to the right tomorrow morning and this time just be sure…But those, you can't tell if it's three or four running points of light; how many times I tried to count them, but they move so fast that the eye doesn't have time to make out how many, after all, they are. This is the panel of the CD player on which you drive discs when you feel tired or sick and want to lie down in bed for a little while to good music, closing your eyes, and not thinking about anything. And here, by the way, you just think that it's been a long time since you ordered any new CDs by mail, and the advertising booklets that fill your mailbox every day tell you in detail about an infinite number of fresh recordings, every second of which you would love to listen to…Tomorrow morning, you will have to fill out the coupon from the booklet and drop it in the envelope sent in the same booklet at the post office…Well, you just have to…

And that green peephole over there is a computer sitting on a corner table. The screen, of course, went out, as it should, in order to save energy, and this light tells you that even though the screen went out, the machine is not asleep and on the lookout, and if you just move the mouse a little, as soon as the screen lights up, and all the endless possibilities will come out on it in the form of small icons that you scattered on the screen in the corners just to look different from everyone else—and even column on the left or a line at the bottom. Then you remember that just today, you forgot to check your mail before going to bed. But it's not enough to get up because of it…So tomorrow, right in the morning…And that red bar over there—it's the one at the bottom of the TV that's lit up. It's burning, but you think with chagrin that you've bought an expensive TV, and you haven't turned it on for God knows how long; you're so tired of the monotonous, stupid chewing gum on all the channels. Or maybe not all of them? There must be somewhere, say, only documentaries about nature are shown—you can watch them endlessly, or musical numbers, or something else neutral. And you still haven't checked everything you're supposed to have on your TV subscription. Judging by the price, this package of channels should be huge; really, you still should be able to find anything for yourself…So you'll have to do it right in the morning…That's a big deal…

That's the darkness now, not just with lights but also with reminders of what you didn't do and what you just have to do the next morning. With this, you fall asleep…And so you get used to this new darkness with lights that you completely forget what it was like once without lights. Here I sat at home one winter, looking out the window at the thickly falling sleet, which was completely plastered over the windows, even without circles and arrows or any other geometric shapes, but just a solid layer, and wondered if I could leave the house tomorrow morning and when the roads would be cleared, and decided to go to bed early. Maybe we'll have to dig up the car in the morning. I lay down, looked at the lights, and fell asleep. I woke up for natural reasons at night…and my heart sank: I was surrounded by a solid, real, dark, like the blackest color, like lamp soot, darkness. And immediately, before I even tried to figure out what was really going on, I was overcome by that real childish horror with all the monsters crawling out of the dark and the rustling under the bed. It was as if I had been a little boy in my old bedroom a good fifty years ago, and my mother had just firmly closed the door, telling me to be a man. Try it here! And it went on—how do I know how long it went on?—enough, at any rate, to make me break out in a cold sweat so that even the pillow and the sheet become wet! Then, however, it let go, and I reached, groping with my hands on the walls, first to the door and then to the toilet. It was already easier to go back, but I couldn't fall asleep again without the familiar lights, and I tossed and turned for a long time, convincing myself that I am really a man and there was no stranger hiding under the bed and in the corners...

And in the morning, the phone rang, and a recorded male voice apologized to me for the fact that the snowfall during the night cut off the electrical wires, and it took several hours to restore the normal course of affairs, that is, the supply of electricity to consumers. The voice also realized that many people did not even notice this event because it happened in the middle of the night when all the good citizens must have been sleeping peacefully. So I was just unlucky...But I remembered what it had been like—the real, lightless, lightless darkness of the past.

Yes, maybe, of course, there is no real sugar, and the summer is hot, but you can definitely see and feel the real darkness at home only on occasion. And even then, without a guarantee. It was gone—the real darkness...As it once was...

The Netsuke from San Francisco

"Any more questions?" asked the session moderator, a man he knew well.

The audience, which had been pestering him with questions for a good quarter of an hour, most of those quite fair, truth be told, was silent this time.

"Now let's thank our friend, Joseph, for his report, excellent and thought-provoking, as usual!"

Having exclaimed that, the moderator turned to the pulpit and led the round of applause, casting a look of his smiling eyes at him. Encouraged by the ovation, he winked back and set out towards his seat in the front row next to the other two plenary speakers who had taken the floor in that session.

"With this statement, we have exhausted the agenda for this morning's session, and I encourage you to peruse the poster presentations in the off-hour before the next session," concluded the moderator.

Everybody started for the doors. After exchanging nods with his acquaintances, he exited the hallway. Everything was going as usual.

To put it straight, the conference wasn't the main reason he came to San Francisco that summer, although he was slated to be one of the keynote speakers there. Or rather, it was just one of the reasons. At the end of the day, there had been plenty of conferences and talks in his life, so he could afford to miss some, especially since he was a bit too old already to tour the country. This time around, it was one big coincidence. Firstly, a long-time friend and colleague with whom he had been close in the USSR and later in the US had settled in Frisco two years prior, and they hadn't met since, even though they would often talk on the phone and exchange e-mails, but a live encounter was still a special thing. Talking on the phone, how could one notice the other having put on an extra pound or two or do other friendly stuff that requires seeing each other, not just hearing?

Then, a familiar netsuke trader from San Francisco called him about six months ago; the merchant knew him well and said that a fine collection would be going on sale just in time for the coming summer when the heirs to a recently deceased aficionado would have gotten all the paperwork straight and begun turning his estate into money. It was, of course, only right that no matter how long some finer things had been lurking in someone's home, even for generations, sooner or later, they would hit the open market, shouldering the eternal process of antique circulation in the world. This collection, albeit mostly beyond his scope of interests, still boasted twenty-something top-notch netsuke pieces, and this trader would be in charge of selling them, so if he managed to show up in San Francisco coming summer, he would probably be able to pick something nice for himself, at a reasonable price, courtesy of the old acquaintance.

Of course, he got stoked right away. Who'd have thought back in the day that he, of all people…Granted, he spent his entire life collecting stuff, and as the years went by, he got set on small oil Russian paintings from what later was called on the West 'Russian Impressionism'. He even managed to carry some of those over to America. The rest came along there; a Chekhov character used to say that everything can be found in Greece, and he eventually found out the US was like Greece in that regard. That's how those netsuke found themselves on the list. Many years ago, he didn't even remember when exactly, but definitely as a boy, he had read, *Krosh's Holiday* by Anatoli Rybakov, a book entirely (if he recalled correctly) revolving around netsuke, those incredibly motley Japanese trifles and for some reason, they got him so hooked that he even recruited a girlfriend of his Leningrader elder brother who helped him find his way into the Hermitage vaults, where he got a chance to see them up close and personal, immediately falling in love…As nice as they were, one couldn't dream of procuring any in Russia. He would time and time again inquire about them in antique shops all over Moscow and Leningrad, but even in those where he was a patron, clerks thought him a madman; one indeed had to be off the rocker to chase something that only ever hit the shelves once in a dozen years, and even then, it would be new stock. Gradually, his dream waned, but little did he know that it was destined to be revived…Upon settling down firmly in America, he rekindled his old Russian habit of browsing curiosity shops and even began frequenting auctions, not yet a big thing at the time, but he would find out that—by golly—those netsuke were so thick there that all he needed was to write checks and go get his old fire quenched. Not really surprising, considering the sheer magnitude of the haul the Americans had looted from Japan. And then the Japanese themselves began flocking to America, bringing their family relics. The only problem was the countless Hong Kong imitations all over the shop displays; one would have a hard time spotting genuine relics among those if one didn't know exactly where to look. Well, it was not the first time this old dog had to learn new tricks. He had put in serious effort, hanging around museums, reading books, and listening to lectures. He eventually developed a fine eye for those things and pieced together a small collection; just one shelf in a glass-doored cabinet housed almost thirty of those tchotchkes, and none of them was junk. Well, of course, he didn't have the funds to afford something patently rare by venerated masters, but even among the second-grade stuff, one could find something that would not be cripplingly expensive but still easy on the eye, something even an expert would find worthy of attention…That was the other bait, in addition to meeting an old friend. And when he also received an invitation to give a talk at a high-profile conference, exactly in San Francisco and just in time for the summer, there were no more hitches. That's how he ended up there.

Just as planned and agreed upon, he came two days prior to the conference to have some time with his friend. And what a quality time it turned out to be! Indeed, something to remember. His friend met him at the airport, and he was pleased to notice all his worries about extra pounds had been groundless; his buddy looked like a pin-up…*Fifty-ish, was he? Damn, he didn't look a day over forty-five!* When in the parking lot and crawling into a brand-new silver Jaguar, he realized his friend's business was also doing just fine—in fact, even better than it seemed when the two were hashing it over on the phone. Sure as hell it was. Exchanging news didn't take too long, seeing as they'd been chewing the rag for a whole hour on the phone just a week before he arrived in Frisco. They already knew full well what was going on, where and with whom. Instead of regurgitating it, they chose to have a grand old time and had a blast maneuvering the silver Jaguar from one winery to another. Two days stormed by. Luckily, they'd made it to his hotel relatively early the day before, and thank goodness, it wasn't the conference opening speech, although he would still have to speak at the morning session. So, upon reinforcing himself with a good night's sleep and a shower, he found deliverance from the endless glasses of wonderful California wines, in which his friend was a great expert, back to scientific affairs, the most important of which—his report, that is—he had just nailed.

And now he was walking, quite pleased with himself, through the hall at the conference center, making up his mind whether to immediately head over to the antique trader or first go downstairs to the grand hall, where, among the many poster presentations, three were the fruit of his lab. He checked the time; it wasn't even noon yet. Good thing he gave his speech in the morning session; he now had the rest of the day at his disposal. The only thing left to tick off was making it to tonight's dinner. Well, that wasn't happening until 8 pm, so no big deal, especially since there would be buses picking up the attendees at the conference center, just one block away from his hotel. He had all the time in the world and thought it would not hurt to check out the poster area, as it was about time for researchers to take posts next to their works, so he had a chance to make sure his employees were up to snuff and had not ditched the crowded conference center—completely indistinguishable from all other conference centers in existence—for the riveting streets of San Fran. It would also be of use to get an eyeful of other posters; there was always room in his head for new smart ideas to stir up his brain a bit. He headed for the escalator. Downstairs, things were as they were supposed to be: all three of his employees stood at attention near the perfectly laid out posters (he paused for a moment to give himself kudos for spending a fortune on printing equipment for his department), and two of them were busy explaining something to other conference attendees huddling around them. Success. And the third one, though standing alone when he came up, was overjoyed to report that their work had sparked great interest; corroborating that claim, he produced a pile of business cards left by those who had asked him for copies of the poster or even the full-text article once printed. The employee was so excited about the universal interest that he asked him to man the booth for a few minutes and appease any potential new visitors while he sprinted for the bathroom. Naturally, he agreed and stood there, side-eyeing the posters on the neighboring stands— nothing of particular interest—and generally staring at things.

That was when she approached him.

"Excuse me," he heard a voice from behind. "Aren't you Dr. Kerner?"

He turned around. Standing there was a good-looking young woman, almost his height; she had a swarthy complexion, with dark shoulder-length hair and slightly slanted hazel eyes.

"I am. You wanted something?"

"Oh, so it's you!" The lady switched to Russian. "May I talk to you in Russian, then?"

"Sure thing," he agreed. "So I reckon you're from Russia as well, right?"

She chortled. "Oh, I get it. A professor can hardly remember each one of their former students! I used to attend your seminars back at MSU, Iosif Aleksandrovich. And we had even discussed some findings."

It was only for one year that he had that workshop going, designed for students working on their theses. He was about to leave Russia, actually, the USSR back then. That helped him estimate her age at thirty-ish, and he realized twelve years was enough for a grad student to change a lot, as he hadn't been able to recognize her.

"I concede I couldn't remember you," he agreed. "So sorry. You were just a regular college girl back in the day, and now look at you; you're gorgeous. Small wonder I couldn't instantly place you!"

She cackled.

"Thanks for the kind words, I guess. It's not easy to get a compliment out of people here. So look, I'm Marina Kameneva. Does this ring any bells?"

"Hang on, hang on a second," he perked up. "Sasha Nikonov was your advisor, right? And at the time, I think, you approached me to ask a thing or two about allelic mutations."

"Exactly. Sasha, check, alleles, check. Seems like your memory still serves you well, huh?"

"Guess what? I was bang on; if it indeed serves, you were just a brat with a ponytail back then and now." It was a suitable moment to admire her, and he got the best out of it. "So, what brings you here? And what's up with Sasha?"

"Here, as in the conference, or America in general?" she inquired.

"Both."

"Well, I had a report to deliver at the conference. Different section, though. And it's been almost six years since I came over. Currently an assistant at Columbia. As for Sasha, though, he chose to stay in Moscow. I think he has quit science since. Used to work for a private biotech firm and then switched to dealing in pharma drugs. I heard he was doing well but nothing more specific. Now you, I know everything about you. There hasn't been a single seminar without discussing some of your papers, I mean, at least the ones that spring to mind."

"Okay, you can cut out the sweet lies. I'm pleased to find out our former students hit the ground running, though!"

The large clock on the wall had almost struck one already, and he thought it was about time to head for the curiosity dealer, but somehow, he wasn't feeling like cutting the exchange with Marina short. It was not like he rarely met attractive women—it was just another big coincidence. The fine Marina herself, the memories of days long past at the college in Moscow, the chance to speak Russian he didn't get often, the hazel eyes, and…

"Listen, Marina," he asked suddenly. "Have you got any plans for the next couple of hours? Like, any business meetings or lunches in the books?"

"Not that I can think of." She slowed down and sounded surprised. "Just wanted to take a look at some posters. Why, though?"

"Care to keep your old professor company for a while? My proposal isn't of the scientific kind, though. See, I'd like to make a run for a local antiquity shop. A forty-minute walk along some of the most picturesque streets from here. There's going to be a bunch of really eye-catching stuff there; I'll fill you in. I don't think I've had the chance to in quite a while. And we can talk about science and our mutual acquaintances from Moscow while on our way. You in?"

"Oh, right." Marina's dark hair was undulated like an ocean wave. "I remember now. People in Moscow used to say you were a famous collector. Can't remember of what, though."

"Famous may be an overstatement; I just love this stuff…I used to collect many things. Not something along the lines of getting my hands on each and every spinning wheel ever made in Olonets Governorate or all of the mid-19th century malachite jewelry boxes, mind you. I wasn't even that big of a collector. I would just get what I liked. It's that I liked a lot of things."

"Like what? Name a few, will you?"

He mused for a while.

"Well, where do I even start…"

"From the very beginning, maybe?" she suggested.

"Aren't you a witty one?" He chuckled and suddenly realized he'd said 'ty' rather than 'vy', addressing her very informally. "Is it okay that I say 'ty' to you?"

"Not only is it okay, but I wouldn't have it any other way, in fact. I'm feeling like a student again. You know, the one with a ponytail."

"Well, if you say so. Let's start, then. The biggest thing for me has always been the books. I began buying them as a schoolboy. Mom used to recollect that's how I would save up my lunch money and hit the bookstores once a week. By the time I finished school, I had put together quite a nice bookcase, even if without any rarities yet. Rarities came in due course. I began buying old illustrated prints and small editions with original lithography. All the more so, as a student, I always had a chance to make some extra cash on the side, so I had more of it to spare. I still would only buy what I really liked, though. Every time I saw a book illustrated by Bilibin or Mitrokhin, even if it was a children's book, I would do my best to snag it. Something by Elisabeth Böhm, not so much. Conversely, a serious collector, well into children's books, would jump at whatever he could lay his hands on. Then I got interested in graphics as a whole, then paintings, and finally, I switched over to curiosities, carved caskets, china plates, and what have you. My place was about to implode with all that stuff. I mean, you have an idea of how tiny those condos we used to dwell in were."

He checked the time again.

"Why are we still here, then? We could well be talking about it all while walking. So, you with me?"

"Sure." She nodded.

"How did you manage to carry all that over to America, then? You left quite a while ago. I thought you weren't allowed to export things like that back then?" she inquired as they were stepping out of the conference center.

"Well, there were a bunch of regulations in place. Some things were allowed; for other things, you needed to obtain a note of approval first, and some were verboten altogether."

"So, how then?"

"Well, at first, I only grabbed a few books and bibelots. I thought I'd never see the rest again, though I didn't sell anything off. Just entrusted most of my collection to my family. Later, with the Union having collapsed, guys like me were de-vilified and allowed to visit, and the laws changed, so I had been to a few conferences, taking back some of my stuff on my way out, some of the thing I just stuck in my bags, and for other stuff I got the paperwork done. Some of the biggest items, I ended up selling them in Moscow, as there was no way they were allowing me to take them with me. Back then, I'd already gained a foothold here in America and resumed my buying habit. Auctions and antiquity traders are all over the place here, unlike Moscow back when I still lived there. So now I've got a proper mess made up of what I'd bought back in the USSR and stuff I got while here. And a fine mess it is. Bits of everything, again. I've even discovered something new and fun since."

By then, they had already passed Market Street and were edging towards the neighborhood where all the antiquity shops were.

"Anyway, I can get on your nerves later with this curiosity banter. For now, though, pray tell, what prompted you to come over? Is your family here with you, too? How did you end up at Columbia? What are you into? I mean—"

Upon blurting that out, he suddenly felt as though he was only interested to hear about her marital status and the rest he had included only to hide, in a manner of speaking, his personal agenda with her.

She didn't seem to have caught on to that and began answering diligently as if she was a student at an exam, "Well, about the decision…I mean, you sure know what was going on with science over there. No money, save for a handful of grants, even those were laughable and only available to the in-crowd. Sasha declared he was quitting science. There was this new joint Russian-American venture, and they made him a neat offer. Me? I wanted to carry on with science, so I kind of had to consider leaving the country. I had racked up a few connections from past conferences, and Sasha vowed to give me a good reference, even though I ended up not needing any of those. I managed to land a postdoc at Yale that left little to want for, and my life was in need of something new, too. I had just divorced at that point. These days in Russia, they call it 'a failed rough draft.'"

"What's a draft got to do with that?"

"Just a code word for the first husband." She giggled.

"I see. My mother tongue keeps evolving. What about the second one? Or should I say, er…the fair copy?"

He had to admit it to himself—he couldn't wait to hear the answer.

"Haven't had luck finding a second one this far. I had already gotten tired of the Soviet people back there, and Americans, while nice, still felt very different. I've got much to adapt to yet, although I'm, you know, in no hurry. I don't think I remember hearing anyone call the second husband a fair copy, but it's been a few years…They might well have coined something to that effect since."

"Okay, let's put this husband talk to rest, then," he said and felt great relief. "So what happened next?"

"I was like anyone else, really; I mean, I had a visa during my postdoc stint, and after applying for an assistant opening at Columbia, I found out they were all over my accomplishments. Over two years, I had four papers published in decent journals as the lead author, and importantly, I'm a female too, and they had a marked lack of women, so they helped me obtain a green card. Been working there ever since. And, even if I were into something, I don't have much time for that. I only go to listen to music, see a show, or a movie when someone takes me out."

Suddenly, he got bitterly jealous. Who were those taking her out? Those Americans she wasn't yet prepared to marry? Just mere dates so far?

"However, I still do alpine skiing. No matter what, every year, I take a week off and head over to Utah or Colorado to spend at least eight hours a day on the slopes."

And then, as if seeing through his screen and addressing his fears, she added, "I don't need anybody there, though. I live and ride all by myself, extending my…you know, battery life for another year."

They roamed the city, and the sun, hiding behind tall buildings, confronted their eyes every once in a while, with window reflections somewhere around floor 15 or even higher up.

"Well, well, well," he said dolefully, squinting at another sunlight onslaught. "Enter urbanization. In these cities, we can't even see the sun, the source of all life, properly, only as a mere reflection. No heat, no UV rays, only blinding light."

She put her hand on his elbow; it sent a warm wave down his spine. She said in an empathic, wise tone he didn't see coming, "Don't you fret. There are still plenty of places to watch the sun as it is. Though this place has its benefits, like those curiosity dealers you're so into. Next time Boston bums you out, go check out Utah. There's more than enough sun in the mountains, but promise me you won't be moaning about not being able to see it *a la naturel* through your shades, will you?"

He moved his elbow to make her hand touch his body.

"Thank you. I didn't mean to whine, honestly. Just showing off my observation skills."

"That's what I figured," she said, making no attempt to free her hand.

They were finally on the right street; he checked the address plaques, *ten more blocks, huh?* and led on towards the shop. Soon he wished they'd flagged down a cab rather than taking a walk. The street went steeply uphill as they proceeded, and even before that, he already had trouble breathing. Unwilling to switch to an old fart pace and talking to her while they walked added to the complexity of the challenge. Not talking to her wasn't an option either, he believed. A pause too long would allow her to begin thinking of something else and maybe even realize she didn't have to agree to this odd, very unscientific trek with this man who was obviously too old for her. And after realizing that, she'd very easily drum up an excuse, like having to get something from her hotel room, or remembering a super important meeting at the conference center, slated to start in exactly half an hour—as the geezer should already be thankful that she almost forgot about it because of him, but seeing as she remembered it in the end, there was no reason to be late for it. He now had to prattle on, stringing his sentences so that he could take a deep breath at every comma and not let her see him pant. He would also strategically stop at select storefronts, drawing her attention to this and that; curiosity shoppes had become frequent, and each one had something worth their refined attention, allowing him to unobtrusively flaunt his expertise again. He knew his lungs would be way less appreciative of rows of lingerie or utensil stores. She didn't seem to notice his struggles, expressing her interest in his comments about ancient maps, Russian icons, or Chinese cast-bronze artifacts. Sometimes, she would even point at things like Tibetan scrolls, asking him to explain the meaning and value of those. It had been going on for about twenty minutes already. Either he was getting used to the rhythm, or he was picking all the right topics for his short lectures, or maybe the pleasure of talking to her and seeing sincere interest in her eyes invigorated his body; whatever it was, his breath was back to normal, his voice took on an assertive tinge, his back straightened, and he stopped imagining her trawling for a reason to get rid of his company. That was when they finally reached the shop where the familiar trader was waiting for the goods.

He stopped at the doors, turned to her, and proclaimed that in order to avoid her getting bored while he'd be all over his favorite toys, he was going to hold a briefing right now so as to get her up to speed with this netsuke business. Looking into her inquiring hazel eyes, he felt he was delivering his speech with eloquence and aplomb, as usual when talking about something he really liked. He told her of the ancient, weird Japanese rules that denied the commoners the privilege of having pockets, so that said commoners had to settle for sticking sundries like tobacco jars and inkwells under their belts; later on, they would invent attaching a string, and a counterweight to those things, so as to swing the leash over the belt and be happy campers. Then, being Japanese, they would inevitably find a way to make those plain pieces of bone, wood, or rock with a couple of holes in them to insert the string into something with supremely pleasing aesthetics. They would carve them into figurines depicting all facets of contemporary Japanese life, from plants and animals to mythical creatures and even full sets of sculpted and scrimshawed depictions of everyday life. Or, well, netsuke.

"For all intents and purposes, you now know nearly as much about this stuff as I do, and the rest will come to you simply by looking at netsuke and feeling them. The more you see, the quicker you'll figure out how to tell good ones from worthless ones, date them reliably, or even place the carver's school. Just allow some time, provided you get hooked, of course. And you're surely fully prepared by now to appreciate what we're about to be shown here. Come in, shall we?"

Hook, line, and sinker—she uttered an antsy "Sure!" and grabbed the door handle.

There was no one in the shop except the old owner seated at a desk in the far corner.

"Hey, Simon!" he bawled. "It's me, Joseph, Joseph Kerner. Remember me? You said you'd got something for me."

"Ah, Iosif!" replied the owner in Russian, for he was a Jew from Minsk who had been brought to the US as a kid soon after World War II and never forgot the language. "Pleased to see you back. You came just in time. I've got a few goodies for you here. And this young lady here, is she after netsuke, too?"

"No, she isn't. Technically, she just wants to take a good look at them. We're colleagues, see, and I've seduced her with talk about your wares, so she figured she couldn't pass up the chance to see it for herself. Would you mind?"

"Would I? Definitely not," Simon certified wisely. "Today, she drops in to look, and tomorrow she'll turn up as a buyer. You're very welcome. Wait a sec."

He snuck into the tiny back room and returned soon, carrying a large, ornate box.

"Here you go, enjoy. We'll get to haggling later."

Simon placed the box on the glass case and opened it. A couple of dozen netsuke were there, cushioned in blue velvet. Already their color, cracked surface, and the way the carving looked exposed their age and hinted there was something in them to warrant a closer look. He reached for a figurine he liked and suddenly realized he had to get Marina busy with something, lest she gets bored. He examined the display and asked Simon to whip one of the trifles out and then handed it over to her.

"Here's a fun one. Old and collectible, is it not? But it tells an amusing story. Try figuring out what it depicts while I'm combing through the box here, okay?" Upon saying that, he put the tiny piece of carved wood into the palm of her hand and turned to Simon.

"Feel free to enjoy them all, Iosif, but I'll have you know I've already got deals in place for all the fantasy and animal ones and for this manjū, too. You wouldn't like the price tags on those; anyway, they're all signed by fine Edo masters, got good provenance, the whole shebang, y'know."

With a sigh, he had to agree with the points Simon made. The pieces were wonderful but way out of his league.

"So what's left, then?"

"These two. Genre pieces, ivory. A fisherman with his catch and a group of schoolboys with a book. Definitely from the early 19th century and very mint. The fisherman is signed, but I couldn't dig up the carver's name. The boys aren't. The man looks like an Edo, and the boys are provincial work but very well executed nonetheless. Genre pieces aren't that popular at the moment, as most have gone fantasy or animalistic. Well, you know how fads are. In a year or two, someone will splurge on a fisherman like that at Sotheby's, and this one will skyrocket, too. But as of now, I'd let you have them at fifteen hundred each."

The price sounded reasonable, and there was still room for haggling, so he agreed to take a closer look. Both figurines were no more than a couple of inches tall and stunning. The old fisherman had a wide-brimmed hat on and a cheerful look in his eyes, his lips smiling under a thick mustache. There was a good reason for him to be all smiles, too, as a large fish with masterfully done scales was swung over his shoulder on a rope, apparently also carved out of ivory; its tail reached almost down to his knees. The dark yellow patina and barely noticeable cracks proved the sculpture's age and added to its charm. As for the two schoolboys, the kids were focused and even frowning and had spent the last couple centuries shoulder to shoulder, hunched over a book on a squat table. He already knew he would be getting both.

"What would you say if I took them both off your hands?"

Simon snorted.

"As one Russian Jew to another, twenty-five hundred for both. And don't try driving a hard bargain. You know well that this is not even a 'loyal customer' kind of price; this is downright friendly."

The old man was telling the truth. He nodded and reached for his wallet.

That was when she touched his shoulder.

"Well," she demanded. "Are you done here? I've been looking hard at the one you gave me, and I don't think there's any hidden meaning to it. A bird is trying to crack open a shell to then eat the oyster. Looks very naturalistic; I didn't even have to think hard to realize that. And the holes down here are probably for the string you mentioned. Is that it?"

"It is, and it isn't." He chuckled. "That's exactly the issue with much of this Japanese stuff. You see the shape of it, but you can't decipher the undertone. Just the surface. This one is exactly like that. You see a bird; it's a hoopoe; note the cirrus, digging its beak into a conch, about to dine on some shellfish, and the scene is beautifully carved and executed. Now, if you knew the symbolism behind it all, you'd pick up on something quite a bit different. In Japanese art, you see, a shell is one of the metaphors for the female private parts; conversely, a bird's beak stands in for the male ones. There's an artist's impression of coitus in your hand, almost a…um…pornographic one. Fun, huh?"

"Well, I'll be!" She wasn't looking the least bit fazed. "That's rich!"

Interesting, he thought, *did I really pick that piece at random, or am I already subconsciously trying to get intimate with her? Looks like I've hooked on, too…*

There was no room for further talk.

"Alrighty then," he said to Marina. "Give me another minute to settle this with Simon and pay up. Then let's take a look at the other antique ones, and then we'll leave, okay?"

"Would you prefer a check or a credit card, Simon?"

"Well, we're buddies, so a check would do, and I'll skip having to pay a processing fee this way, too."

He wrote a check quickly, and Simon began the process of carefully packing the netsuke in a lavish Japanese box. Meanwhile, they were pressing shoulders over other figurines from the big casket, sharing a magnifying glass; her hair brushed against his cheek. He told her about the two sumotori and the hat-wearing skeleton with a staff, explained the Japanese phenomenon of frog impressions being madly popular, and wished for nothing more but to keep feeling her.

"Here," said Simon, handing him the neatly bound box. "Congratulations on a fine addition to your collection. If I get something else for you, I'll let you know. As for you, dear lady, feel free to drop by if you like what you've seen. I'll get you a good piece or two fit for beginners. Goodbye!"

He lamented having to return the box with the remaining figurines to Simon but did it anyway; then he wrapped his arm around Marina's shoulders casually, and they headed out.

"So, what do you think?" he asked. They were outdoors already, and he regrettably had to let go of her.

"Stunning," she said sincerely, then she hooked her arm through his and inquired, "Where to now?"

He checked the time again.

"Oh damn! Time flew as we talked. It's half past five already, and we still have to make it back to the conference center to head to the dinner. We aren't running late per se, but I'd rather take a cab from here. Especially because it's rush hour already, and we might get in a jam."

"Well, if you say so..." Did he really hear a slight protest in her tone?

He hailed a cab and gave the driver the destination; they got in the back seat, and the car took off. Their thighs were touching, and they listened to the music coming out of the car stereo. He recognized Sting and uttered suddenly, *"Goi sidyat i slushayut Stinga."*[1]

"You're even versed in these things. Impressive."

---

[1] 'Гои сидят и слушают Стинга', lit. 'Goyim are sitting there, listening to Sting', is a line from Декаданс, lit. Decadence, a song by Agata Kristi, a Russian rock band active since 1985 and especially popular in the late 90s.

"It's been quite a few years since I've been living. I just keep stuffing my head," he said plaintively.

"Oh, knock it off, using your age as a compliment bait!" She suddenly put her hand on his and even petted it. "You still look exactly as I remembered you from the seminars!"

"I wish I did." He sighed.

Enjoying Sting's tunes and small talk, they didn't notice the fact that the car was approaching the conference center already. He suddenly realized that the box holding his new netsuke was still there and said, "You know, Marina, I don't think it would be too handy to carry this box around at the dinner. What would you say about stopping by my hotel to drop it off? It's just outside the place where the buses will be waiting for us. Get it to my room, grab a swig of water, and off we'll go. How's that for a plan?"

She faltered for a moment, and he felt his mouth getting ash dry.

"Fine," she conceded after a few seconds. "If you say it won't take long…"

They got out of the cab. He took her by the hand as if unsure whether she might yet change her mind and make a run for the hills. They took the elevator to his room in silence. He unlocked the door and invited her in.

"You better get seated." He pointed at an armchair by the window. "While I'm unwrapping these netsuke and setting them on the table. I want to admire them again later. Care for a drink after such a long walk? The mini bar is full to the brim."

"Actually." She smiled. "The other way around. May I use your bathroom? After the long walk and all."

"Oh, sure thing! Feel free to!"

He gestured invitingly towards the bathroom door and felt as though this perfectly routine request had created an air of nearly familial intimacy in the room.

She locked herself in the bathroom while he stood in the middle of the room perplexed, trying to figure out what to do next.

"Gee, whiz! I don't even remember what a man is supposed to do in such a situation. Twenty years ago, I'd ram the bathroom door down or jump at her as soon as she was out. But now, what if she gives the old goat face-washing instead? That'd ruin this wonderful day for us both. I'd hate allowing her to leave just like that, though…And there's definitely interest in her eyes when she looks at me…So what am I…"

He didn't have the time to finish his train of thought as, at that moment, she returned, walked up to him, and cast him an expectant look.

"So? Are you still planning to head to the dinner, or?"

He checked his watch for the umpteenth time.

"There's still quite a while before the buses depart. Do we need to hurry? Let's stay and chat some more. So, the thing about netsuke is…."

Her facial expression was indiscernible. She kept silent.

Good God, what are you doing? Cut out the netsuke crap already! She knows what's going on as well as you do. What an idiot…Just go for it. Hug her!

But he couldn't just go for it without any words.

"Listen, meaning no offense, may I ask something very personal?"

"Sure," she replied softly.

And he went for it.

"What's your opinion of casual or, shall I say, extemporaneous hookups? Like, if two people feel they might have a good time together, and—"

An involuntary desire to insure himself against the potential negative answer, which could, of course, be just a nod to the tradition or an essential part of a game being set up, but would still require him to rethink his assault tactics or even retreat to save face, scared of whatever his bad habits and stupid folly could bring upon him, made him add hastily, "Just don't say you won't hear about it! Even if so, you'd better laugh it off, lest you lose the fleur of a modern-day woman with not a care in the world and reinforce my inferiority complex...."

She cackled.

"I won't be ruining it, then. Or laugh it off or reinforce your self-doubts. I'll put it straight; it depends on the man, the mood, and the setting."

"That's a lot of variables! So I get that it's a rare occurrence when the man, the mood, and the setting all come together. What would you say, then, if the man was me, the setting this very room, and the mood, well, you tell me...."

"I'd say that it's indeed a rare occurrence."

He felt disappointment and relief—an odd combination—but she didn't allow him any time to try and decipher this nuance. After the shortest pause, she moved along, looking him straight in the eye.

"But right now and right here, the mood couldn't be better, the man is downright charming, and even the setting is favorable enough."

She smiled. And there was no going back.

He delicately put his hands on her shoulders and gently pulled her closer. She half-closed her eyes, offering her lips. He pressed his own against the corner of her mouth. That was when she finally embraced him. He felt her firm breasts touch him, and with arousal in full swing, he began kissing her properly. She was at first reluctant to respond, but little by little, she opened up, and he felt her tongue in his mouth; her hand on the back of his head was busy pressing him close. Still locking lips, they had instinctively begun working on each other's clothes, and now their hands were already flying free, tearing off buttons, clips, and straps, getting them out of the way, and with each article hitting the floor, they were inching closer to the king-size bed. He stuck out his hand to remove the blanket; they descended on the sheets, and he felt her tight, swarthy body merge with his own. The rest was like a wonderful dream; he only regained his senses after her soft moaning had culminated in a short, bird-like shrill. He still couldn't tear himself away, slowly rubbing his lips all over her hair, face, shoulders, and breasts. He caught his reflection in the large mirror on the wall at one point; seeing the disheveled graying locks, festoons, and deep creases on his cheeks almost made him retch, and instead, he opted to admire the sight of her again. Enjoying the wonderful imagery, he felt as though the messy-hair-festoons-creases guy had left, and the one still here was himself from the days when she and her ponytail were sitting in front of him at his seminar.

I wonder, he thought to himself, *what she's seeing. I sure hope I look like the man from twelve years ago to her, too.*

Gradually they winded down, and now they were just lying there, her head resting on his arm.

"Mommy would always caution me against going to hotel rooms with men!" she exclaimed suddenly in a breaking voice. "Everybody knows what happens next."

"Implying you're regretting your choice?" he inquired, startled.

"Just kidding!" She chortled. "What's there to regret? I fell for you all the way back when you were my professor."

"Is that so?"

"It sure is like most other girls. We'd always argue about who was going to be the lucky one, but it was like you never noticed. No one got lucky in the end, I assume?"

"That's correct," he assured. "I wasn't the smartest back then."

"That's what I'm talking about!" she said with delight. "No one got lucky but me. It's been a few years, but I still won!"

"Some prize I am," he sneered skeptically. "Just a gross old thing."

"You have no idea what you're talking about." She brushed him off. "These days, men aren't old unless they've hit seventy. You've still got plenty of gas in the tank."

"What would I need it for, though? Talking ears off cute things like you and sinning with them?"

"Sinning, huh." She giggled. "My granny, quite a piece of work in her heyday who had affairs all the way into her sixties, used to say it was only sinning as long as your legs pointed at the ceiling. And as soon as they're down, away goes God's frown. Mine are down, so I'm no more sinning, see? It's also up in the air who kick-started the sinning. It was me who first approached you, remember? The American way. Just like the girls from Sex and the City."

"Can't say I know much about that show. Don't think I've seen it at all. Well, if you say it's like the movies, then so be it. Just spare me some self-respect, okay? I'd like to think I also had a role in this play. Didn't I do my diligence, using those endless inane stories to seduce you?"

"That you did," she agreed merrily. "And the seduction part worked to mutual gratification, too. Listen, what about the time, then?"

"Well, if you're going to hit the dinner, then it's time. I've changed my mind about going there, though. It'll be all talk, noise, and crappy food, as usual. Would you rather go have dinner with me? I know a joint or two nearby. Top-notch places, those. And we could return here afterward. Thoughts?"

"Well, dammit!" She seemed upset, and he wanted to believe it was natural. "I'd absolutely love to, but I've got two meetings to attend there. We're planning a collaboration with San Diego, and there's a lot to discuss. As for the other, there's a dean from Michigan who wanted to talk to me about transferring there, with a promotion, no less. I'd like to find out about the terms they're offering. And I've got a flight back early in the morning, so I'm going to have to check out of my hotel at six. I wish I could've known."

"That's fine. You definitely shouldn't skip out on meetings like that. I understand. We've had most of the day to ourselves, so let's try being thankful for that. I won't be going anyway. You'll be busy, and I've already met everyone I needed to meet. I better sit here, catch my breath, have a quiet dinner somewhere, and think about you. Now you'd better be getting ready."

She kissed him on the lips, got out of bed, and started picking up her clothes off the floor. He was ogling her unabashedly; she intercepted his stare and asked, "Could you not look, please? Making me feel uncomfortable."

"Come on now!" he protested. "You're absolutely gorgeous, and I haven't had time yet to admire you in the entirety. I only had the chance to feel or eyeball some parts of you. Don't do that to me. I want to remember you well."

"Well, how could one object after being flattered like that? Ogle away."

Grabbing an armful of clothes, she made her best impression of a model on a catwalk while retreating to the bathroom while he was getting an eyeful of her.

In fifteen minutes, she was ready. By then, he had put on most of his clothes as well. She approached him, gave him a hug, pressed her cheek against his, and whispered, "See you at some other conference, okay? Keep me posted on your plans, and I'll try to make something happen. If you're up for it, I mean. Me? I've had a magical time."

He replied, also whispering, "You bet I'm up for it. And I'll definitely keep you posted. You aren't getting off this hook anytime soon. Mistreating old people is a bad thing to do."

"That's another thing my mommy used to say. I won't, I promise!"

She licked him in the ear, pulled away, and disappeared behind the door with a wave of her tanned hand. Beautiful, businesslike, successful, and still so young. What are the odds?

He wandered about the room aimlessly for a while, picked up the blanket, looked out of the window, and turned on the TV, paying no attention to what the news anchor was mumbling. Then he noticed the box on the table, which he never got around to unpacking. He sat at the table, looking away from the window, untied the elaborate bow, pulled the blue velvet pouch out of the box, and loosened the drawstring. Out came two more pouches, also blue but smaller, and those produced the figurines, carefully covered in soft wrapping. He removed it and placed the pieces on the table, feasting his eyes upon them.

A sudden ray of evening sunlight, one of the last ones, struck the windows of the skyscraper across the street and rebounded to end up plum in the middle of his table. In the short moments, while this light was there, he noticed the schoolboys still huddled over their books, caring for nothing else in the world but the old man with a fish in his hands met him with a youthful smile; he could swear the geezer winked at him.

He Did Not Remember the Name of That Little Town...[2]

He was indeed struggling to recall the name of that little town where it all ended. They weren't even going to make a stop there. They just wanted to drive through it by the evening and then stay overnight in that fancy motel eighty miles away, touted by the real estate agent who was helping them search for a new home. When they entered the town, the fight was already in full swing, so he didn't even notice the town sign, much less on the way out. So he never found out whether it had happened in Zeleny Park, Chistye Vodopady, or Malenkie Peshchery. He never ditched the habit of translating all those countless Green Parks, Crystal Falls, and Small Caves into Russian, even though she would taunt him about it. So, he did not remember in which of them, scattered along the plains of Nebraska, he was left alone in the car, and well, alone overall…On the positive side, at least the century was a certainty and not just that. December 12th, year two thousand and two. It all started

---

[2] 'Я не помню, как звали этот маленький город', lit. 'I do not remember the name of that little town', is a line from 'Бедная Птица', lit. 'Poor Bird', a song by Nautilus Pompilius.

around 7:00 p.m. and ended around eight something…A little over an hour, and fifteen years of their life disappeared, as if it hadn't happened…

They'd been driving for six hours…And that's only counting that day, the second after they'd left New York, and on the first, it had been almost ten hours non-stop. He wasn't even sure if it was worth the drive—it'd surely be easier to take the plane. But, on the flip side, they saved a ton of money this way, especially considering there were two of them. It would be more convenient to have a car upon arrival, to browse around the neighborhood and see where they had to dwell now and get a ballpark idea of the housing situation…By the way, it was all about that offer he had received from a local firm in Nebraska that had licensed several of his patents from the university where he worked. The company seemed set on capitalizing on those patents, so he allowed them to convince him to leave the university in New York and step up as head of the firm's R&D. The terms, it goes without saying, were better than what he could've asked for, that is the paycheck, the share allotment, and the lab…Of course, he would only have to do what the company required of him from then on, but on the other hand, it would be more than enough for the rest of his life. Not enough for a Nobel, mind you, but at least it wouldn't be a drag…No reason not to give it a go in one's late thirties. However, he had no clue how his wife would react to such a change; she was enamored with New York, but she would also nag at him all the time about his poor life and career choices or less-than-ambitious approach to money. The new endeavor would give her a chance to make up for all that. Anyway, no point in guessing—there she was, together with him in the car, and she'd spent the whole day yesterday talking about what house they would be able to afford on his new income, what she could do in this godforsaken Nebraska, where they would spend their vacation, and if there were any friends living nearby, which is to say, under three hours away…Then they spent the night at the planned hotel, and the first day was up…And now the next one had rolled around. One more sleepover, and by the next midday, they were supposed to arrive. Meetings and conversations with people from the company would ensue, and then the time would come for them to tend to their own affairs. Thus, the schedule was set…

But things were somewhat tense in the car that day. It's not that something crucial had been said or done, but everything, including her tone, her facial expressions, and even her silence, felt odd, as if a single misplaced word was guaranteed to spark what had been happening more and more often in the old house in New York. He remembered how during their night at the motel, she would roll around and mumble something barely comprehensible but with a flavor of true annoyance so loudly that it even made him wake up a couple of times, just in time to hear another dissatisfied utterance. In the morning, she had been trying hard to avoid locking eyes with him. When, after breakfast, he'd set out to carry her bags to the car and make the payment, he noticed her sitting in the lobby, talking to someone on the phone, or rather listening, her face very focused, as if at that moment something really important was being decided upon. Was she having trouble at work or something? After they'd gotten a move on, he made sure not to start any new quarrels, keeping silent and listening to the music coming out of the car speakers…Or thinking whether something had been wrong between them in New York or how to right that 'wrong' when in Nebraska.

A Nautilus[3] CD was in the player, and he was pondering and recalling things to the tune of *Skovannie Odnoy Tsepyu*[4].

She'd been mad for quite a while. Come to think of it; she may have had the right to be. As it would later become obvious, they had emigrated for his sake so that he could continue his scientific career in a decent place while she was supposed to stay by his side. They hoped things certainly would not turn out worse than what they had in Moscow. And since there was a job offer from New York, it was probably going to turn out a fair bit better. After all, NY, the capital of the world, is faring way better than the Moscow of the late Perestroika era, with the tearsome plight of science, savage early businesses, and a new breed of mobsters and thugs recklessly driving on the sidewalks in their supercharged Mercedes sedans. NY was no worse equipped with theaters, music halls, and galleries than Moscow, or even better, implying there should be no problems finding a way to spend the downtime if there would be any. And in a case of a sudden nostalgia rush, Brighton Beach, familiar with the few American movies and publications that had reached the Russian audience,

---

[3] Nautilus Pompilius, also known among fans as simply Nautilus, or Nau, is a cult Russian rock band, formed in 1982 and led by the singer Vyacheslav Butusov; their songs featured heavily in the 90s and early 2000s Russian movies, such as Brat and Brat 2.

[4] Title of a song by Nautilus Pompilius, lit. 'Chained Together'.

would be right there for them, providing instant deliverance from homesickness. In a way, that's what happened, but keeping her 'by his side' didn't last. At first, he would go to the university, and she'd run rampant through the shops, getting a fill of what she'd never had before, but there are limits to even how long one can enjoy shopping. She was young, full of energy, and with a fine head on her shoulders. Six months' worth of stores and TV was clearly enough. She'd restocked her wardrobe nicely, and it was time for a break from all that. A word here, a line there, a bit of hearsay, and she'd found herself attending the course for junior programmers, seemingly a far cry from her past life as a history teacher at a public school. Long story short, it turned out that all her past career choices had been grave mistakes, and she declared herself a born programmer. She managed to finish the course in a single year rather than the planned two, and her instructor helped her land a nice gig at a large company, despite the lack of any stateside work experience. A year later, she was already running a team of system administrators, taking home a heftier sum than he ever was able to earn. Not by a landslide, but still. For some reason, this fact came to annoy her, even though back when it was him who had been providing for them both, and she had not even entertained the idea of taking the course, this situation seemed to her somewhat natural, causing nary an objection. She didn't decide to take the course because he insisted on it or because they were stone broke. She just grew tired of doing the chores, chaperoning guests around New York, or staring at the TV. It simply played out the way it did. By then, she was proficient enough to never again be left unemployed anywhere, and the company he was having negotiations with mailed them a list of potential employers for her, promising their most active assistance in landing her a job. She could still be a woman with a serious job if she so wanted, and finding things to spend her salary on would really not be that big of a challenge…

He himself had gotten carried away working in New York, especially since the goings were, to be quite frank, exceptionally good; research grants were rolling in, his papers were a success, his team was extensive, and he was making rounds across all of America with conference talks and keynotes. He could honestly think of nothing else to strive for, and it did not even occur to him that such things as promotions existed or that he could've fought for a better salary every year, not only by the four percent that the inflation rate dictated but for much more, as long as his success and authority allowed it. One should take into account that his mindset was shaped in that vintage brand of the Soviet Union where the salary of a lab-leading professor at a decent institute was set in stone at 500 rubles a month from the approval date to the very retirement, and no higher rank existed unless, of course, said scholar would suddenly choose to switch to an executive job, but that was usually reserved for those who yearned to make up for certain research failures. Here, by contrast, he was his own boss, as he was the one who obtained the grants; all he had to do was work. Working eight to eight, no end in sight; one needs to allow extra time to undergo changes. That luxury he didn't have.

'Eta muzika budet vechnoy[5]', promised Nautilus.

Especially since he had a kind of second occupation; way back in the day, in Russia, he would sing songs of his own penning and play the guitar. Somewhat of a minstrel, he was. And that even got him some degree of popularity; he would feature at all meetings of homebrewed singer-songwriters, tour colleges, and even had a vinyl out, albeit the songs that made it were considered by himself utterly boring, but as pros would say, they 'worked'. And so they worked their way onto the vinyl. Later on, when the issues at his lab, which was struggling to stay afloat, along with the entire ship of Soviet science, consumed his thoughts, leaving no room for songs, his music gradually withered. Here, though, with the work hitting the highest gear once again, the songs reemerged. They came flooding in; regardless of his being swamped with work, they'd swarm in his head. That was a veritable torment; single words, lines, or even entire stanzas. They confronted him everywhere; when he was parked at his workstation, sitting in front of the TV, crawling out of his car, or, worst of all, at night. It seemed to him as though the verse he'd given birth to at night had been exceptional, bristling with elegance, purity, and authenticity. He would smile in his sleep and even wake his wife up with joyful giggling or excited moaning; he believed he was waking up and writing them down, but in reality, they were getting wasted…Anyway, what he was able to scribble down at day felt enough. Except there was no one to sing for. He stowed

---

[5] Эта музыка будет вечной—title of a song by Nautilus Pompilius, lit. 'This Music Will Be Eternal'.

them away for the future. For some reason, she was very annoyed with all this noise; she saw it as an attempt to build a bridge into the past, the past she had chosen to cross out. She would sometimes push him at night and inquire angrily. "Look at the time! What on earth are you laughing at? What's so freaking hilarious?"

He would just turn over and keep on listening to the words in his head, lying with his eyes closed, smiling quietly, drooling all over his pillow…

'*Mi budem zhit s toboy v malenkoy khizhine*[6]', Butusov was imploring.

"She'd have to be out of her mind to agree to that!" she commented suddenly. "One should live in a decent house, not a cabin!"

Since the remark didn't concern him personally, he chose to stay quiet and went on reminiscing.

Well, it wasn't just about the songs. She suddenly began getting pissed at all sorts of things. The fact that he had been working till late at night and had no time to go check out the movie everybody was buzzing about at work. Her desire to invite her mother from Moscow to stay with them for some six months while they only had a three-room apartment, so her arrival would put everyone in discomfort. The fact that some mysterious friends of friends had gone on a cruise to Alaska while all they did over the years was a trip to that crummy Santa Lucia, and even while there, he was on the

---

[6] Мы будем жить с тобой в маленькой хижине (lit. You and I, we will live in a small cabin) opening line from the song 'На берегу безымянной реки', lit. 'On the Bank of the Nameless River' by Nautilus Pompilius.

phone with his lab for three hours a day. The fact that he was always at some other conference while she was reduced to sitting at home bored was where he should have realized that she 'would no longer tolerate being bored'. There had been innumerable issues like that, difficult to object to, seeing as her initial assumptions had been so wrong. She had to understand—just had to—that his salary depended on grants, right? And getting enough of those required spending twelve hours a day in the lab, sometimes longer. They made it to the movies often enough, and should they have missed one, it wouldn't be that much of a whammy; they could rent a tape later. Didn't she appreciate their luxury condo in downtown New York? Well, it would be her who'd raise hell if he entertained the idea of leaving Manhattan to get something twice the size for the same money. Moreover, touring Alaska next year was on their bucket list already, and as for the conferences, his career would lose half the momentum should he stop attending them. And what did she even mean by 'would no longer tolerate being bored?' It was beyond unambiguous comprehension!

And she would come up with more and more examples of her acquaintances who had their working hours set in stone, whose wives didn't have to work, who never skimped on jewelry, didn't binge on vodka with blockheads in ripped jeans like himself, knew their way around dressing up, and never disgraced their special ones, and if they happened to have any hobbies, it would be something decent: either alpine skiing or yachting or even gardening, but not batting out idiotic songs no one wanted to hear. Those were people with decent lifestyles, unlike him and, by extension, her.

She would insist time and again that she didn't even need all that; she simply craved attention, which he deprived her of while she, in fact, was more worthy of it than most…

He would laugh it off or tell her off, and while she never said it outright, it occurred to him more and more often that everything they had been doing together for all these years had just ceased to interest her, and whatever he'd roll by her at that point wouldn't make her happy.

It would seem that suddenly everything she wanted was coming together: the working hours should now be regular, barring some emergencies, of course. The salary was to die for; he was getting allotted a neat share that, provided everything went as planned and the company went IPO in a few years, was guaranteed to rake in enough for them (and even their children that he still hoped to have) to never again pinch pennies. Even their grandkids would most likely never want for anything, except maybe diamonds, should they decide to take up collecting those. The company agreed to fund the purchase of a large house for them as per one of the transfer conditions, and even his new job title had a nice ring to it, compared to the puny 'research professor' (for some reason, it was eating away at him; no one fully understood what this title entailed, but clearly it was something leaving much to be desired!). In other words, all they had to do now was to enjoy themselves!

The stereo was blasting a medley of Nautilus songs; now, the recognizable tune of *Krylia*[7] began. When he heard

---

[7] Крылья—title of a song by Nautilus Pompilius, lit. 'Wings'.

it, he involuntarily muttered the familiar line, *'Gde tvoi krilya, kotorie nravilis mne....*[8] '

He slightly turned towards her while keeping his eyes on the road.

"Listen, did I tell you about that wonderful thing I saw recently at that conference in Frisco?"

She kept quiet.

He went on, "Seems like I didn't. There's a picture by Joel Witkin in their contemporary art museum. He may well be a celebrity, though the name doesn't ring a bell with me. Anyway, that piece is a blast. Called 'Woman once a bird', it's a photo of a woman who's got a tight metal belt with a padlock around her waist and wounds on her shoulder blades that look like she used to have wings, but they were torn off. I wonder what came first, those lyrics for Nau or Witkin's pic? Similar ideas, those…Bang on. Women do have wings that come off at some point in their lives…Shame that—"

"So you're longing for my wings now!" she erupted. Before he could offer an apology, claiming he was just singing a familiar line that dredged up this memory, never meaning to refer to their previous conversations or her own situation, singing or talking about that picture from San Francisco. To be frank, he didn't even consider the meaning of the words when he sang them; they just burst out, and then Witkin's work followed naturally. She continued aggressively, "That's it! No more wings for you! They wore

---

[8] Где твои крылья, которые нравились мне, lit. Where are your wings I used to love so)—a line from the song 'Крылья', lit. 'Wings' by Nautilus Pompilius.

down! I've flown my fill! That's enough! There are young airheads for you to fool with your teenage romance. Get some tears out of them with this trite bullcrap. Me? I'm done here."

He knew this tone well. Her voice would take on a tinny sound, and she would not look him in the eye—granted, sitting in the car side by side, locking eyes wasn't easy, but the tone was there…There it goes…Still, he wasn't getting a clue that this conversation was about to get serious; he even tried to shrug it off with a joke, "I feel offended that you think my range of interests is so narrow! I'd be no less happy to sing you some Morrison. I like him, too. 'Show me the way to the next whiskey bar. Don't ask why, don't ask why…' Does that work for you? Actually, why don't we pop into some bar on our way? A shot wouldn't hurt right now, huh?"

But she wasn't easy to put down; she seemingly ignored his rebuke and moved along, "And I can't bear to hear this Butusov of yours anymore! Along with that Soviet nostalgia of yours. We've been driving for two days, and I haven't heard a thing except for your Nau and all sorts of Russian pops, nothing! Was it even worth coming to America if all you wanted was to get buzzed off all the trash you could very well listen to in Moscow till the cows came home? And I thought you'd gotten fed up with all that noise there. You were the one to uproot me. You! And don't you dare tell me otherwise? Working there was no longer an option, you said. Your scientific scene was dying, the mood was getting on your nerves, and people had turned into cattle…Am I missing something? I kept listening and finally got persuaded. Well, let's go for it, I thought. He'll have a good job there. Better odds, a wonderful mood, and no thieving mugs in sight. And just like that, you got a job, you got breathing room, and the mugs around you are now all honest. Just live! Why the hell aren't you letting go of everything you've left? You keep drinking your vodka with Soviet leftovers like yourself, and you only watch Russian TV, getting kicked out of *Banditsky Peterburg*[9], and even in your car, all you've got is this Nautilus. It's driving me crazy as we speak! You made me believe in anything you burbled. I was dancing to your tune all the way…Now it's over!"

"Look," he attempted to cut in. "What are you even talking about? What does Nautilus have to do with this? And even if it does, why didn't you say so sooner? I could play something else…"

"Right. Alisa ('Алиса', lit. 'Alice' is a cult Russian rock band active since 1983, led by the singer Konstantin Kinchev) or something along these lines."

"Why, Alisa? There's a whole bag of CDs at your feet, and not even a third of those are Russian. The rests are American bands or classical music. Just see for yourself. Aren't you and I going out to listen to music often enough? Is that also Soviet nostalgia when Russian performers come to Carnegie Hall? They travel all around the world these days. They don't really have any nationality, except for the place they pay taxes at…And we go to exhibitions all the time. Only two or three were Russian over all these years. We've got plenty of American buddies, too! Why are you

---

[9] 'Бандитский Петербург', lit. 'St. Petersburg of the Gangsters', was a popular Russian TV crime drama of the early 2000s.

suddenly mad that I sometimes hang out with my Russian friends? Wasn't it you who always said it felt nice to keep the good traditions of an uncivilized country after moving to a civilized milieu?"

"Was it me, or was it not? You have such a way with words that I sometimes don't recognize my own points. If it was really me who made them, anyway…"

"Do you mean to say I'm lying to you, or what?"

"Once again, if it was indeed me who said that, I must have put a different meaning in these words. Whatever! This all doesn't matter!"

"What does, then? Why are you all riled up?"

"Because you don't want to embark on a decent life!"

"What do you mean, decent? What is this all about?"

"Most everything! Everyone else I can have decent, straightforward dealings with. You're the only one with quirks. I have a really hard time getting what's on your mind."

"What kind of quirks? Care to explain? Name some of those you've got decent dealings going on with?"

'Ya tak hochu bit s toboy',[10] insisted Nautilus meanwhile.

"I have decent dealings with whoever is a decent person! You have no idea there are people out there who live decent lives, do you? Ones with decent schedules, ones who have the time to take a woman out to a decent place, ones who live in decent-sized houses, and ones who have

---

[10] Я так хочу быть с тобой, lit. 'I so much want to be with you', is a line from the eponymous song by Nautilus Pompilius.

decent hobbies without getting bees in their heads. That's whom I can have a decent relationship with."

"Wait, wait, do you mean to say you've gotten yourself someone who dwarfs me, a decent enough man? You sound like you're with someone already like you were comparing me to him…With me trailing, obviously…Are you serious right now?"

"Am I serious? Are you an idiot? Is this your blasted 'ni komu ni kabelnost'[11] in play again, that you can't see a thing until it hits you in the face? Sure as heck, I'm with someone! And not someone like you with your asinine 'you and I in a little cabin' stuff. He's a decent American guy with decent American habits and decent things to worry about. He never departs into the Perfect White[12]. He never sits on the hillside, either[13]. He's working, he's earning cash, he's got his daily graft to attend to, and he knows what a woman wants!"

He was completely baffled.

"Are you for real? Or are you just messing with me to drive me mad? Why?"

---

[11] Ни кому ни кабельность, from Russian 'ни кому', lit. 'to nobody' and 'некоммуникабельность', lit. 'incommunicability, social awkwardness', which can be interpreted as 'Incom-unique-ability', is the name of a live album by Nautilus Pompilius.

[12] A reference to Абсолютное Белое, lit. Perfect White, a song by Nautilus Pompilius, and 'уйти в синее', lit. 'Depart into the blue', a Russian idiom meaning 'to get blackout drunk'.

[13] A reference to 'Мы сидим на склоне холма', lit. 'We are sitting on hillside', a line from the Люди на Холме, lit. People on Hillside, a song by Nautilus Pompilius.

Nautilus was singing *'Mi zhivem v gorode bratskoy lyubvi'[14]* when she came back with a retort that, if anything, was absolutely devoid of love.

"Wake up, you bozo! Don't you understand what I'm saying? No more jokes! We've had our fill of fun…And I have no intent to drive you mad. If you don't get it, then so be it. But I want to be with the man who gets it."

His heart missed a beat. He knew she was telling the truth. At that instant, everything he had deliberately ignored rushed into his head. It was like a dam had collapsed, and his mind became flooded with glimpses of everything that had been wrong with their life. He remembered her being absent most nights, claiming to have gone to see one girlfriend or another, to catch an evening sale or a party at work. What was up with those girlfriends, sales, and parties that held her until midnight on a weekday? Or with all that new jewelry she convinced him she'd bought on deals from a rundown store? Well, that could be true, but lately, she would wear those all the time. Even when he'd ask her to put on something he'd bought her, she would laugh it off or outright refuse to do that, as if she hated to have any material signs of his attention on her. And that hostile reaction to anything he'd done, said, or offered…It was going to ridiculous lengths. He remembered a recent occurrence when they were crossing a street together; the red had just kicked in, and he grabbed her hand. 'Careful, you don't want to get run over, do you?' he said, just to see

---

[14] 'Мы живем в городе братской любви', lit. 'We live in the city of brotherly love' is a line from the 'Город братской любви', lit. 'City of Brotherly Love', song by Nautilus Pompilius.

her tear away and yell, 'Piss off, will ya?!' then dash straight into the upcoming stream of cars. The driver of the nearest cab had to do a wild swerve to avoid hitting her, yelling 'bitch!' out of his window as he did.

He was pondering and recalling things while she blurted out an enraged sequence of hollers about some guy named Jeremy she should've long dumped him for, the apartment cluttered with Russian books she was so tired of, and the size of the said apartment, which was three times as small as those of their friends with comparable incomes. She lamented the fact that his workaholism only manifested itself in coming home to eat and sleep, never converting into anything that raised or improved his quality of life, a problem that mysterious Jeremy didn't have. She orated about having been right when she refused to have an early child; she insisted that anything borne of his loins would be American only by birth while being ridden with any Russian inferiority complex one could think of; she piled allegations upon allegations that all fell in line with what he imagined an angry woman would be bringing up. Should she have made a point to prove to her man and herself that her decision to split had been right, even if, some of the said allegations were far from accurate…And, apparently, it no more made any difference that they had been together through some long, hard times…

'To a woman, there is no past. Once love ends, you're a stranger to her' (A line from Loneliness by Ivan Bunin, Russian poet, and Nobel Prize winner), he remembered suddenly with a kind of chuckle.

"Are you not listening?"

She was almost screaming at that point.

"Why would you think so?" he uttered calmly and even somewhat indifferently. "I'm listening. I get that this Jeremy, more like Jeremiah, or even Eryoma, if he were a Russian, is set on supplying you with service and, er…personal comfort on a level you fully deserve but I could never provide. And here it all comes; you just have to grab it. One would be a fool not to. Especially seeing as we know now, you've been so busy lately, evaluating this Eryoma's personal skills while benching me in case this plan of yours falls through. Gotta have your bases covered, at least until the next Eryoma comes up on the radar. Anyway, it seems like you've got everything going for you, so the time has come to brief me. See? I've been listening and heeding what you offered."

"You've always had irony to spare," she asserted cattily. "Well, your irony is going to get you into hot water one day."

"I assume I've gotten into it already. Anything to add? The only thing I don't think I get is why you had to drag this out or even make this trip with me. Couldn't you have said it back at home and saved yourself the trouble of driving through half the country? Or did you want to make absolutely sure that whatever I was going to get wouldn't touch what Eryoma had in store for you? Or maybe you'd drop the talk should it turn out the other way? And then, I gather, he called you and vowed to outbid me no matter what, which is why you chose to stop wasting your time…And the rest you poured on me. I mean, come on, you don't give a damn anymore; you just want to arrange things the way they'd make me appear guilty of everything in your eyes…As though it was me who pushed you to the limit, and you had no other choice but to find yourself an affluent, wise American man. I wonder what you'd be blaming me for if it was another Russian emigrant instead. For forgetting my pedigree in forgoing vodka in favor of bourbon? Or for putting our hypothetical children in danger of losing their Russian roots by preferring Eric Clapton to Nautilus?

"Pull over," she said suddenly in her regular voice.

"Seriously? Right here?"

"Here's as good as anywhere else."

"And what are you going to do here on your own?"

"I'll figure it out. Just got to find the bus terminal, and the rest is none of your business."

"Granted, it's not, but I feel obligated to get you to the terminal, at least. Don't hop out here. Somebody might assume you're trying to escape an abusive husband, bursting out of the car like that, and call the cops on me. Then I'll have to languish away the night in the box while they're getting things straight, and I've got to be at my business meetings tomorrow and call the real estate agent. See, I can't afford to go behind bars today…So, pray, bear with me for a few more minutes."

At first, she was silent; he believed she was dallying with the idea of furnishing him a sleepover in custody. But then she thought he was right.

"Fine. Find out where the station is and head straight there."

"Hang on a minute…Seriously, care to explain why you even went on this trip when you were having it so good with this Jeremy already?"

"I wanted to give you one last chance, but you blew it."

"What chance? What exactly did I blow? It was all going just as we planned, wasn't it?"

"Enough of this chit-chat. Pull up here and go ask someone. You don't dig it now, and you never will!"

She was right in assuming that he never did…

He hit the brakes and rolled down the window, letting a burst of fluffy snow into the car. He addressed a guy in a long-hooded coat, "Could you please direct me to the nearest bus station?"

"Someone's arriving?" asked the man warmly.

"More like departing, actually."

"I see…Drive two blocks straight ahead, make a left, and then three blocks more. You'll see some buses there; that's where our station is."

"Thank you so much!"

He rolled up the window and slammed on the gas. The station was right where the local said it was. There was no more talk in the car. Only after opening the trunk he inquired, "How are you going to repack your stuff, then?"

"Don't need to. It's all in this bag here."

He realized she'd prepared for this in the morning already, packing a separate bag. It wasn't about some ephemeral blown chance at all.

She grabbed the bag and headed to the ticket office without looking back.

All that was left for him was to get in the car and take off.

In the wing mirror, he saw her whip out the phone and dial someone.

"Looks like she's in a hurry to tell Eryoma about her deliverance from all issues and declare herself his rightful prize. He might even throw a meet and greet party for her…Well, all the power to them."

The last track on the Nautilus CD was *Stranniki v nochi*[15], a fine song if he ever heard one! The player switched to the next one. He would always cram the discs into the changer at random, so he had a moment of curiosity before finding out what followed Nautilus. He heard Jim Morrison's voice—what a weird coincidence; hadn't he just recalled one of his songs when talking to her? *Interesting*…Nau and Doors indeed had something in common.

Well now! It just isn't true that I only ever listen to Nau. I'm well enough versed in the local culture, too. Better than she does, at any rate, he thought to himself in a huff, as if still having that conversation with her. As if such a minor thing still mattered after all that had happened. Even before it did, such an observation would only make her throw another tantrum, as it would make her feel as though she'd been erring—unthinkable!

Just why did she have to pull the plug on their shared history this evening and not some other day? Why would she even want to leave New York with him? She'd spare them both much time and pain had she told him what's what and left for her American beau right there. They weren't the first nor the last to live through this…But no, she was happy to discuss the plans, order him around when packing, engage in all sorts of banter while in the car, or even keep peaceful silence until it all went downhill to the tune of

---

[15] Странники в ночи, lit. Wanderers in the Night—a song by Nautilus Pompilius.

Krylia. What was even her issue with Nautilus? Or was she still keeping the option to turn the tables until his unfortunate singing outburst? It happened soon after Eryoma called her, so she might have thought he was suspecting something—well, one had to be an utter moron to overlook all that had been happening. Would they now be heading over to settle in their new home some 200 miles out of Omaha if he hadn't sung that line from Krylia and brought up that picture from San Fran? He was never able to find an answer to that.

He never saw her again.

He transferred what he owed her through the attorney.

He doesn't even remember her face anymore.

He even suspects he won't recognize her even if they run into each other.

'I po ulitse proyti i drug druga ne uznat...'[16] ('И по улице пройти и друг друга не узнать', lit. 'To walk along the street without recognizing each other...' A line from Stranniki v Nochi)

His car shot its way out into the snow-covered fields, leaving the lights of the town's farthest gas station behind; darkness fell all over him. It was snowing heavily, and huge, shapeless, frozen flakes kept sticking thickly to the windshield, only to be wiped away immediately. The headlights were the only bright spots on the road, lane striping blurred by the snowfall; when another bump would make the car jump up, the road would become invisible for

---

[16] 'И по улице пройти и друг друга не узнать', lit. 'To walk along the street without recognizing each other', is a line from *Stranniki v Nochi.*

a split second, and myriads of snowflakes would block the light's way before it dissipated into the pitch-dark blizzard, unable to highlight a thing as if the headlights were off…And there he was, alone in the endless sea of white…The last man in the entire universe…

Jim Morrison agreed in his unique manner:

'When the music's over, turn off the lights…'

www.ingramcontent.com/pod-product-compliance
Lightning Source LLC
Chambersburg PA
CBHW050541160726
48003CB00002B/694